Piper
to the Clan

Also by
MARY STETSON CLARKE

The Glass Phoenix
The Limner's Daughter
The Iron Peacock
Petticoat Rebel

Piper
to the Clan

MARY STETSON CLARKE

The Viking Press

New York

❧ FOR HELEN CLARK FERNALD ❧

Map on page 73 by Joshua Tolford

First Edition
Copyright © 1970 by Mary Stetson Clarke
All rights reserved
First published in 1970 by The Viking Press,
Inc., 625 Madison Avenue, New York, N.Y.
10022. Published simultaneously in Canada by
The Macmillan Company of Canada Limited.
Library of Congress catalog card number:
71-102925. Printed in U.S.A.

Fic 1. Scottish history

VLB 670-55661-0
Trade 670-55660-2

1   2   3   4   5   74   73   72   71   70

Contents

CONTENTS

Author's Note

Ever since the autumn day twelve years ago when I first visited the Scotch-Boardman House in Saugus, Massachusetts, I have been haunted by the account of the Scots who lived there after being taken prisoner at the battle of Dunbar on September 3, 1650, and sold into seven years' service to the Saugus Iron Works.

In the raftered attic of the ancient house I fancied that I could hear the ghostly voices of those departed Scots, and from that moment on I felt compelled to dig back into history to reconstruct their story. In a novel for young people, *The Iron Peacock* (Viking, 1966), I chronicled their arrival and first year in Saugus. In a nonfiction account, *Pioneer Iron Works* (Chilton, 1968), I told more about their employment at the Iron Works.

With the unearthing of each new fact, I grew more and more curious about the background of these Scots, until finally I knew that I must go to Scotland for further study. In September of 1968 my husband and I drove east and

7

south from Edinburgh, retracing the Scots' route to their defeat at Dunbar and their subsequent tragic march through Berwick, Alnwick, Morpeth, and Newcastle to Durham.

At Dunbar we visited the Reverend J. S. McMartin, M.C., M.A., and Mrs. McMartin, to whom we shall ever be grateful for their cordial hospitality. Mr. McMartin had for years made a study of Dunbar's history, with special attention to the battle of 1650. He guided us through the old town, ruined castle, and battlefield, its open slopes little changed after three hundred years.

During fireside hours in the manse, Mr. and Mrs. Mc-Martin shared with us their considerable store of Scottish lore. Later Mr. McMartin procured information from the Scottish National Library in Edinburgh for my use, and was kind enough to go over my manuscript in scrupulous detail.

Although the story is based upon historical fact, its characters are wholly imaginary. Kindonal, Ross McCrae's boyhood home, is also fictional. However, both the people and the area are representative of Scotland in the turbulent days of the seventeenth century.

The march of the Scots southward from Dunbar to Durham has been reconstructed from a study of documents and accounts combined with a careful inspection of the captives' route and places of imprisonment. From time to time, as we stood in the shadow of castle walls or beside battered effigies, the veil of 318 years parted, and we felt as if we were in the company of the survivors of that earlier desperate journey.

The recent designation of the Saugus Ironworks Restoration as a national historic site may stimulate new interest in the history of those hardy clansmen who worked off their seven years' indenture as part of its labor force and then, as free men, established homes and families throughout New England, contributing significantly to the growth and development of the United States.

Again I was at curst Dunbar
And was a prisoner taen,
And many weary night and day
In prison I hae lien.
    SIR WALTER SCOTT
    Minstrelsy of the Scottish Border

Ross McCrae

Puffs of white cloud scudded across a sky brilliantly blue on the morning of July 22, 1650, as Ross McCrae walked eastward along the rutted road skirting the Firth of Forth's southern shore. He covered the ground rapidly with a Highlander's bold stride, his long legs moving in effortless rhythm beneath his belted plaid, his head with its thatch of dark hair thrown back as he took great gulps of the salty air.

How deeply he had missed the freedom of hill and shore he had not fully realized until yesterday, when he had been sent from crowded Edinburgh and the chafing confines of army camp to Tantallon Castle for a tally of its men and arms.

Somewhere in the confusion of dismissals and appointments, while Scotland's leaders sought the most loyal and godly men as officers for the Army of the Covenant, the inventory for Tantallon Castle had been lost. And thankful Ross was for that mischance. For here he was, on as bright and sparkling a day as had ever dawned, walking free and unmolested, with no veteran of the continental wars barking orders at him as if he were a levied Spanish peon or Flemish farmer. How could any officer, even though he had fought under the great Gustavus of Sweden or some other European monarch, put more faith in training and drilling than in a Scot's fierce loyalty to chief and clan?

Beside Ross trotted his collie dog, Tam, one ear pricked skyward and sharp nose lifted as he sniffed the fresh morning air. This is almost like old times, thought Ross. We might be tramping along the shore of Loch Ruich at the Laird's bidding to visit the herders' crofts and to learn what goes well or ill with the folk of Kindonal.

Only the land was different. Unlike the deep glens and steep crags of the Highlands, the Lothian plains, rich with oats and barley, rose in long sweeps to the hills of Lammermuir, where flocks of sheep dotted the distant slopes. And just ahead was a fishing village, its sturdy houses a far cry from the rude bothies of the northwest coast of Scotland. Had he taken the right turn for Tantallon, a mile or so back?

By the roadside two small boys vied in a contest over which could jump farther over a broad puddle. As Ross drew abreast one said, "When I'm a man, I'll be as tall as Fingal."

Ross smiled to himself. Even here in the south of Scotland lads were raised on tales of the legendary giant and his deeds.

The second boy stretched his small frame upward and flexed a spindly arm. "I'll grow sae big that I'll—I'll—" He paused as if searching for some preposterous feat, then finished with a triumphant smile, "I'll build a brig to the Bass, and ding doon Tantallon."

His companion snorted. "Not e'en a giant could smash doon that castle," he said contemptuously.

Tantallon must be nearby, thought Ross, for boys to talk of it thus. Farther on a knot of men were gathered at the market cross. He would inquire of them.

As he came up to the group he heard one old fellow say, "She told that she dreamed the castle would fall."

"Not Tantallon!" said another, with a short laugh.

"Aye, that's what I heard. She said that Cromwell's men would take Tantallon."

"No soul with a lick o' sense would believe that Tantallon's walls could be breached," a loud voice claimed. "Only a witch would say sich."

"Och, a witch she maun be then," an old man stated, wagging his white beard. Others nodded their heads in agreement.

Ross felt a chill running down his spine. A soldier should not be tormented by echoes of an old woman's screams as she was dragged to the stake. He thrust aside the memory of the witch-burning two weeks ago at Edinburgh and called out, "Can ye tell me, am I on the richt road to Tantallon?"

The circle broke, and the men faced toward him, staring at a strange face. "Follow this road, and ye canna miss it," the white-bearded elder said brusquely.

Ross sensed their eyes on his back as he walked away. An unfriendly lot, these Lowlanders. At home a man would offer to show a stranger the way and would give him the gift of his company. These folk seemed to begrudge even the giving of directions. Was it because they lived close to the Border marches? The land hereabouts had been fought over so many times, its inhabitants might rightly look with suspicion upon a newcomer.

When he had left the village behind, and the road ahead loomed empty, Ross reached for the bagpipes slung over his shoulder. Shaking out the sheepskin bag and pipelike drones, he blew into the slim wooden mouthpiece. This would be a good time to practice the march his father had taught him a few days past. This time he must try to get the tune right. But even as he filled the bag with air and tuned the drones he knew that for all he was the seventh of his line to pipe, he could never equal Black Donald's robust notes, no more than he could match his father's bold good looks. He placed his fingers over the holes in the chanter, and the first notes of the march came forth thin and reedy. Tam, barking sharply, darted across the road and snapped at the gulls that swooped in from the North Sea. The next moment he ran toward the sheep grazing on a far hillside.

Ross watched him go. Tam isn't all hunter nor all sheep dog, he thought ruefully, but a little of both. And it is the same with me. I veer one way as the Laird's ward and kinsman and the other as Black Donald's son. While I'm sitting at the Laird's side as he judges what penalty a man shall pay for stealing one of his neighbor's sheep, stray tunes sing in my mind and take my thoughts off the judgment. And when I'm piping a tune, I begin to question if a chieftain should rightly have the power of pit and gallows over his clan.

But here he was again, letting his thoughts wander. Pressing the swollen bag snug under his elbow, and fingering the chanter afresh, he set his mind firmly on the march. Now the notes sang bravely in the breeze. Soon he came to the difficult part, where the tune seemed to double back on itself and then go forward again. He ran through the melody once, then repeated it. Ah, now he had mastered it, and when he was at camp again he would play it for his father and hope for his approval.

Swinging the pipes back over his shoulder, Ross quickened his pace. He had met no travelers since leaving the village. The countryside was so quiet it was hard to realize that Scotland was on the verge of war and that English troops might any day cross the border, ready to strike.

Soon the road wound close to the shore, only a narrow ribbon of green separating it from rocky cliffs that dropped sheer to the sea. How blue the ocean was, with white caps frothing, and gulls and kittiwakes soaring and screeching above it.

Offshore about two miles rose the steep contours of Bass

Rock, standing like a craggy sentinel at the mouth of the Firth of Forth. Ross chuckled, remembering the small boy's boast. Only a giant like Fingal could build a bridge to that rocky islet.

Soon he must glimpse Tantallon. Would it resemble the castle of Kindonal where he had spent his boyhood, its stonework golden beside the blue waters of Loch Ruich? Or would it be a fortress as black and grim as Stirling or Edinburgh Castle?

Ahead the road rose abruptly to climb a steep hill. Coming down its slope toward him was an old woman. One clawlike hand held her shawl close about her thin shoulders. The other grasped a long stick with which she was driving a gaggle of geese. Wisps of gray hair blew about her face. Ross's throat tightened. Might she be the woman the man had called witch?

Tam ran up and barked sharply at the hissing fowls. Ross gripped the dog's thick ruff. "Quiet, Tam," he ordered, and the dog was silent.

The old woman had cheeks like shriveled apples. She waved her stick and called out, "Ho, laddie, ken ye the price of geese in the town?"

Laddie, indeed! Couldn't the crone recognize a man when she saw one? A man on a mission for General David Leslie? Pulling himself up to his full six feet and trying to look older than his seventeen years, Ross asked indignantly, "Nay, and why should I ken aught o' geese?"

Her cackle rasped in his ears. "Many a man will do murder for a taste o' guid goose before these troubles be o'er," she said darkly, and hobbled on.

Ross looked after her uneasily. Do murder for geese when the fields were thick with grain, when dovecots swarmed with pigeons, and sheep grazed on the hills? The woman must be daft—or worse. The quicker he put distance between himself and the old harpy, the better. He started up the slope.

At the top of the hill he forgot the woman completely. Ahead loomed a castle, its red sandstone vivid against the blue of sky and sea, its bulk majestic atop a high cliff. On this vast promontory jutting out into the North Sea, its walls rising to breathtaking heights, Tantallon appeared impregnable indeed. No wonder men and boys alike were certain it would never fall.

Tantallon

For a mile Ross strode forward impatiently. With each step he took, the castle seemed to grow more lofty and massive. And by the time he had turned into the well-worn road to Tantallon's outer ramparts, he felt dwarfed by its steep bulk.

Before crossing the bridge that led over a deep ditch to the castle's outer gate, Ross called Tam to him and commanded, "Begone!" The collie fixed his gaze on his master for a moment, lifted one ear as if to show he understood, then ran off and disappeared behind a low hill.

Though some men kept their dogs ever with them, even in the kirk, Ross had long since taught Tam to go out of sight at his command. There were some places where even a well-trained dog was a nuisance, and Tantallon could be such, especially if the castle dogs were jealous guardians. Tam would not venture far, Ross was certain. And when he left the castle, the collie would be waiting, plumed tail waving a welcome.

Two men lounged at the arched stone doorway of the high gate. One honed a halberd's point; the other munched on a piece of cheese.

The man with the weapon rose. His beard was gray and his smile quizzical. "What might be your errand?" he asked.

Ross stiffened. How his drillmaster would scoff at so unmilitary a greeting. "I'm frae General Leslie's headquarters," he said.

If the guard was impressed he did not show it. "And I suppose ye have proof o' the same?"

Ross drew a folded square of paper from his saffron shirt. "This is for Captain Alexander Seton," he said impatiently, and started forward.

The man shifted his halberd so that its point was no more than an inch from Ross's chest. "Wait till I've looked at it. Then I'll judge whether ye may enter." Beneath the soft voice was a steely edge. He inspected the folded sheet, his outer lip thrust forward. A moment later he turned toward a third soldier seated at an iron-studded inner door and bawled, "A visitor for the captain. Escort him."

The escort led Ross into the outer bailey, a spacious courtyard bright with sunshine and the flashing of birds' wings around a dovecot. The garrison would have plenty of fresh meat during the winter, thought Ross, eyeing the pigeons.

Ahead the barbican towers rose menacingly before a curtain wall so lofty it seemed to meet the sky. As he passed over the drawbridge, Ross could see the deep ditch it spanned. Overhead hung the portcullis's iron teeth, black and threatening. When he stepped inside the grim entrance, the heavy walls seemed to press down upon him. Awed by the mass of stone, he followed his guide through a shadowy tunnel pierced by doorways, each occupied by an armed guard.

Abruptly they emerged into a broad, sunlit inner court. Ahead and to the right were low walls stacked with fodder. Behind them was the mid-tower, flanked by broad stretches of curtain wall and two more towers, one to the east, another to the west. From the west tower stretched a row of stone buildings.

The inner courtyard had all the activity of a village. Through an open door Ross could see a baker pulling loaves of bread from an oven. Not far away a blacksmith was shoeing a horse while another smith hammered out a pike head on an anvil. Men sat about in the sun, burnishing armor.

At a well, two boys turned a windlass to bring up dripping buckets of water. And nearby a half dozen women scrubbed laundry in a long trough, their tongues as busy as their hands.

While Ross watched, a young girl came up to the women, a bundle of clothing in her hand. Fair hair hung limp about her face, and her eyes were downcast. "It's sae brisk a day for drying I had thocht to do my wash," she ventured.

The women looked up, and as if at a signal, spread their

arms along the trough's edge. One with bristling red hair spat venomously at the girl's feet. "There's no room!" she jeered.

The girl cowered and retreated toward a doorway. Two men were passing. At her approach they shrank back against the wall as if they feared her long skirt might brush against and contaminate them.

Ross's guide said impatiently, "This way to the Long Hall." He hurried along the base of the western curtain wall to a doorway just beyond the west tower. Up a curving stone stair they climbed to a landing on which a door stood ajar.

Ross could see a large chamber lighted by small arched windows on the courtyard side, with a hooded fireplace and two long window slits on the outer wall. The escort turned and descended the stairs, his duty done. Ross waited uncertainly outside the room, loathe to interrupt its occupants.

A stocky man with iron-gray hair and a bristling mustache, evidently Captain Seton, was striding up and down, talking with a gentle-faced woman seated in a ray of sunlight. Her hand was poised as if she had left off her embroidering to listen to him.

"What more proof do ye need that she's a witch?" the man growled. "Didna the gateman's bairn sicken and die after she kissed it? And ye were the one told me of her dream that the castle would fall."

The woman's eyes widened in earnestness. "Kettie confided in me only sae that we might save ourselves. Ye have no right to condemn her for a dream. Ye have nightmares aplenty yerself."

The man stamped his foot. "But Agnes Sampson was not *my* grandam."

"It's sixty years or mair since Agnes Sampson was put to death in Edinburgh. Can ye not forget the puir soul?"

"After she put an evil spell on Earl Angus in this verra castle? And caused his death? She deserved well the fire and the stake."

The woman rose and put a hand on her husband's arm. "But Kettie is not her grandmother. She is as innocent of evil as I."

The man placed a swift hand over his wife's mouth. "Let no one hear ye voice such madness."

Ross waited to hear no more. He lifted his hand and knocked on the doorjamb.

The captain swung to face him. "Well?" he asked impatiently.

Ross stepped forward. "I bring a message from General Leslie," he announced. "I have orders to take inventory of your force."

Captain Seton thrust out his hand. "Gie me the letter," he ordered. "I need nae young upstart to tell me its contents."

Flushing, Ross obeyed. A minute later he stepped back as the captain gave an angry oath and shouted, "I sent a full count to Edinburgh not two months ago. Think they I've naught to do but scratch wi' pen and ink?"

Ross cleared his throat. "I could make the report."

The captain laughed. "Leslie writes that I'm to make a list of my force and arms and return it by his messenger." The way he said *messenger* made Ross feel that there could be no lower rank possible.

"I'll take ye wi' me and ye can do the scriving, since ye're sae eager," continued the captain. "We'll start in the Douglas Tower; 'tis nearest." He started heavily down the stairs, each thumping footstep a protest.

The woman caught up a sheet of paper, a quill, and a small pot of ink from a table and gave them to Ross. "Pay no mind to the captain's temper," she said. "He has reason enow to be wrought up." Her smile restored some of Ross's confidence.

In the next two hours Ross was thankful that he had not been ordered to take the inventory alone. Even the simplest task, counting the men and officers, he could not have accomplished unaided, for there was a constant coming and going through the honeycombed fortress. He would have been hard put to locate even the many cannon. As for classifying them, he would have been at a total loss, for here were culverins in three sizes, as well as cutthroats and slangs. In addition there were many handguns, a few of the new flintlocks, but more of the old matchlocks, and even some hackbuts and harquebuses.

After the inventory had been made, Ross was left alone to struggle with his scribbled notes. By late afternoon he had composed a reasonably neat list which numbered a total of fourscore men, eleven officers, a dozen horses, sixteen great guns, and one hundred and twenty small arms. He took the paper to the Long Hall and presented it to the captain, who scowled over it and scratched his signature at the bottom.

Ross folded the list, put it in his shirt, and was turning to go when the woman spoke. "Will ye not ask him to tarry the nicht, husband?"

Captain Seton rubbed one hand across his forehead. "Och, aye," he said. "Tantallon turns no man out in the dark. Tell the guard ye're to sup and sleep here."

What was left of the afternoon Ross spent watching the two smiths. Uncanny it was what they could do with a bar of iron. First they heated it to a whitish glow, then beat it with heavy hammers. Next they thrust it back into the fire, which was made to burn fiercely by means of a bellows operated by a boy. Then came more hammer blows, more trips back to the fire, and at the last, there was a Lochaber ax with a long narrow blade and a hook at the end for catching onto a man's armor and unseating him from his horse.

A page came running with an iron cuirass. The tasse at the bottom had come loose, and his master wanted it repaired. There was a muttered consultation, the armor was heated, and the smiths went to work. They bent so closely over the metal that Ross could not see exactly what they did. But in a short while the skirtlike projection was firmly in place, and the page bore the breastplate away.

A smith as skilled as these would be useful at Kindonal Castle—far more so than the gnarled man there who made a botch even of shoeing a horse. Ross wondered if the Laird had thought of having one of his men trained in such work. He might speak of such a possibility on his return to the camp.

Beacon
Fires

The fresh fish and peas ⟩and newly baked loaves were welcome at sundown, as was the talk of the men-at-arms. Some had fought with the Parliamentarians at Marston Moor when Cromwell had led his forces out of what seemed sure defeat into a triumph of victory.

"Old Noll is a man I've no stomach to meet in battle," said a gray-haired guard. "Not for naught is he dubbed Ironsides."

"Is that why ye came here instead of Edinburgh?" taunted a lean-faced stripling.

The guard jutted out his chin. "And what's wrong wi' wantin' to be inside strong walls?"

"The walls won't save ye if what Kettie says be true," said the stripling with a laugh.

"Blast the witch! She'll bring a curse on Tantallon yet. Mark my words." The gray-haired man raised a warning hand.

Later that night Ross tossed and turned wakefully. After

weeks of sleeping in the open, he found the guard room stuffy and the snores of his companions anything but soporific. He rose quietly, picked up his bagpipes, flung his plaid over his shoulder, and tiptoed out into the court. No moon lighted the cloudy sky, and only a lone torch sputtered at the entrance to the middle tower.

Ross made his way toward the east tower, and started up the curving stone staircase. After a few steps he was in complete darkness. No matter, the steps were solid, though worn and uneven. With one hand on the wall, he moved upward.

At each landing Ross stopped to listen. All was silent. Four stories he climbed and came to the top of the great curtain wall. A guard, his shadow darker than the night, was moving along the high path. Not wanting to be ordered back to the guard room, Ross waited for him to vanish into the mid-tower, then climbed up to the platform roof and settled down behind the corbeled parapet. Here was fresh air, here was quiet, and here he was alone. Now he should be able to sleep.

He stretched himself out, wrapping his plaid about him against the sea damp, and waited for drowsiness. It did not come. Instead he felt wide-awake and wary, as if something were about to happen.

There's nothing to fret over, he told himself. My work is done, and by morning I'll be on my way back to Edinburgh. But still his uneasiness persisted. When a stifled cough sounded nearby he was not surprised, only angry with himself. Because no one had challenged him, he had assumed that he was alone.

"Who's there?" he growled, his hand on the dirk at his belt.

"Only me," whispered a small voice. "Kettie."

"The witch?" he asked, the hair on the back of his neck prickling. In his mind's eye he could see the old woman with her shriveled-apple cheeks.

"I dinna feel like a witch though they call me one." The voice was unmistakably young and filled with despair.

He had heard those tones before. Suddenly he remembered. "Ye're the lass that could find no place to do her wash?"

"Ye saw that?" Her tone was wondering. "Ye maun be the Highlander come frae the general."

"I am," he assented. The girl had some sense if she recognized him as a man of the Highlands. Almost at once he was on guard again. Witches had a way of knowing things, and from what he had heard in the Long Hall, this Kettie's grandmother had been condemned and burned.

"When did ye first ken ye might be a witch?" he asked.

There was a sob. "When I had the dream of the castle falling. I could see the walls, all battered, and the captain's face when he stood on this very tower and called out in surrender."

"What about the babe that died?" he asked. "Did ye put a spell on it?"

The girl burst out weeping. "I loved the bairn. I wished it no harm."

"Why did ye not speak out and say so?" he asked.

"I did. But folk pointed and shouted at me, and made signs to ward off evil. And then I began to think"—the voice dropped so low that Ross could scarcely hear—"that perchance I might be different."

"Ye look like any ordinary lass to me," said Ross stoutly. "Why do ye think ye differ from ither folk?"

"Because o' my dreams. And sometimes I see things ahead."

"Why do ye not leave Tantallon?" Ross asked.

"Because I've no place to go."

"No kinfolk? No friends outside these walls?"

"Nay, none. And besides, of what use would it be for me to leave? I know that I'm to die here."

"Nobody knows how he will die," said Ross.

"I know what my death will be. I saw myself in a dream, falling down a cliff onto rocks, and the sea carried awa' my body. The cliff was like that at the seaward side o' the castle."

Ross was silent. The girl sounded as certain of her fate as if she had sure knowledge of it. If she was not a witch, she was headed for trouble, talking this way.

"Hae ye told anyone about this dream?" he asked.

"Nay. I dare not talk to castle folk now."

Ross stood up. "I'll gie ye some counsel," he said, "and

ye'll do well to take it. Leave Tantallon as soon as ye can. Ye could live elsewhere, perchance in Edinburgh."

She gave a low cry. " 'Twas there my grandmother was killed."

"Well, somewhere else," he said impatiently. "But get ye away from here, and stop sich feckless dreaming."

Ross was turning toward the stair when suddenly his eye was caught by a pinpoint of light on a distant hilltop. The spark flared in the black night, grew to a flickering flame, then swelled to a mighty blaze.

A beacon! One of the fires lit to warn Scotland that the English had crossed over the boundary and were even now in the Border marches. Soon there would be fighting. He must get back to Edinburgh and the clan.

Toward the west another tiny pinprick glowed in the blackness. By now the Laird, his father, and companions-in-arms would know that the English were on the march. There would be other fires ignited on craggy hills to the west and north until the alarm went out over all of Scotland.

A cry sounded from the curtain wall. "The beacon!"

Torches appeared in the court below. Men ran sleepily from the guard chambers. Footsteps thudded on the stairs, and voices rang in the rooms.

The girl stood beside Ross. He could feel her trembling. "Dinna fear, lass," he said. "Ye'll be safe enow within these walls."

Just then a guard burst upon them, a torch in his hand. Swift as a greyhound the girl slipped past and started down the stairs. The terror in her face was so great that Ross followed.

They had reached the lowest level when the girl stopped at a slit in the wall. Ross halted behind her and put his eye to the narrow opening. In the courtyard was gathered a band of women, muttering and gesticulating. At their head was the red-haired dame of the laundry trough.

" 'Tis that Kettie has brought this harm upon us," she shouted.

"She should be chased awa'," offered a stout female.

"And free to set her spells on other innocent folk? Nay. Let her die as her grandam did—and good riddance!" The woman waved the torch, her mouth working in frenzy.

"Like her grandam, at the stake?" quavered an older voice.

"Aye—at the stake. Witches maun needs be burnt." Shrieks and shouts echoed the cry.

"We maun find the witch!"

The crowd started to move along the eastern curtain wall. The girl's slender frame was quaking. Listening to the mob, Ross felt none too steady himself. He must act— and quickly. Soon they would come to this tower.

Shaking out the folds of his plaid, Ross put his left arm around Kettie, pulled her close, and wrapped the woolen folds about them both, covering her from head to ankles.

33

"Do we walk in the shadows," he said, "wi' ye on the dark side, ye'll nae be seen."

Hidden in the tartan's length, the girl matched her pace to his, step by step, along the courtyard's edge to the mid-tower. A group of guards were gathered there. Ross hesitated.

A soldier looked up and said, "Oh, 'tis the Highlander. If ye're wantin' to get back to Leslie ye maun wait till the morn when the drawbridge be let doon."

Ross turned and walked slowly back toward the east tower, then set out beside the low wall that bordered the seaward escarpment. Far below, the sea beat in distant surf. He could feel the girl trying to hold him back.

"Go not here," she whispered frantically. "Not by the cliffs."

" 'Tis the only way," he said firmly, "if I'm to take ye to Mistress Seton."

He could feel her yielding to his direction and knew he had been right to think of the captain's wife, just as he was right in his decision to skirt the unlighted side of the court in order to reach the Setons' quarters. He could hear the captain's voice booming out from the ramparts. His lady would be alone, and might give the girl succor.

"Let me walk on the inside, awa' from the cliff," begged a muffled voice.

"Ye'll be in mair danger of being seen there," he said. "Hold fast to me. I'll no' let ye fall."

The crowd of women had grown. Surely there were more

than a dozen now. In addition there were a few men, their fists and voices raised in anger. Ross quickened his pace, then slowed. He must try to appear like a man merely passing time till the dawn.

The night wind was cool upon his face. Forcing a saunter, Ross marched his swaddled companion around the borders of the courtyard. Undetected they passed the sea gate and the outward walls. Ahead lay the bakehouse and kitchen, both empty and dark. Then he saw that the crowd had turned and headed for the foot of the Douglas Tower, the very place that he must go to enter the Long Hall.

While he paused, Kettie plucked at his sleeve. He saw that she was peering through a gap in the plaid. "In here," she whispered, and led him up a short flight of steps just beyond the kitchen. It went to the back entrance of the Long Hall. Above was a broad doorway. At his knock it was opened by Mistress Seton, a candle in her hand.

The
Haven

Before Ross could say a word, Kettie tumbled out of the plaid and to her knees before the woman, her eyes wide in terror.

The captain's wife looked at Ross. "I canna keep her here," she said, and stooped to smooth the girl's fair hair. Then she straightened, listened a moment to the cries in the courtyard, and beckoned them both to follow.

Ross put his arm under Kettie's and urged her along behind Mistress Seton through a doorway into a small chamber at the end of the Long Hall, next to the Douglas Tower. She pushed aside a tapestry on one wall, disclosing a door which she unlocked with a key that hung from her girdle.

"Ye maun go down those stairs," she said, pointing.

Kettie shrank back against Ross. "Not to the dungeon!"

The woman smiled. "Do ye think I would send ye there? These steps lead around the dungeon to the old haven where small boats used to find shelter. It was partly destroyed in a storm, and has not been used for sae many years that scarce any know of it now. Once ye are down, go alang the beach until ye be out o' sight o' the castle. At first light climb the cliff and go to my old nurse at the cottage on the Broxburn in Dunbar, just off the Great Road. Take her this so that she will know it was I sent ye." She unclasped a brooch from her bodice and pressed it into the girl's hand.

Captain Seton's voice sounded in the Long Hall. "Ho, wife!"

"Go now!" Mistress Seton gave Ross a shove. He stumbled onto the stairs, Kettie behind him, as the door swung shut. The darkness was blacker than any he had ever known. Thoughts of Tam waiting near the outer gate, the clan in arms without him, the message he bore for Leslie, all whirled in his mind. Then he felt Kettie's fingers, cold as ice, on his arm. Only one thing mattered now, getting the girl safely away from her accusers.

He started to take a step, tripped on an end of the plaid, and almost fell. Frantically he yanked it over his shoulder next to the bagpipes and hitched his belt tight around the folds. Then he put his hand out to the cold stone of the wall and began the descent, the girl clinging to his back like a limpet.

The steps were of rough stone, uneven in height, but steady. For that he could be thankful. One slip and who knew how far they might fall?

Round and round, down and down they went, like two

ants on a corkscrew. He could feel himself growing giddy with the circling motion. The walls grew colder and were wet with slime. The air was heavy with moisture. How much farther must they descend?

Ross halted to clear his spinning head, then continued down the steps. Suddenly he stepped into ankle-deep water so icy that he almost cried out. At the same moment his hand met the rough planks of a door. His fingers raced over the wood and found a heavy bar swollen with damp. Heaving with all his might, he raised it and pulled the door inward. In a moment he and the girl stood in a hollow space at the foot of the great cliffs.

Together Ross and Kettie clambered along the shore, putting distance between themselves and the castle. Over rocky outcroppings and shallow beaches they made their way to the northwest, the night seeming less dark after the blackness of the stair well. At last they rounded a steep crag. Now we cannot be seen from Tantallon, thought Ross, and he helped Kettie climb up on a large boulder. Its top, broad and dry, must be above high water. He eased himself onto the rock and let out a long breath. So far, so good. Beside him Kettie was shivering.

"What might ye be afraid of now?" he asked impatiently.

"I'm cald," she said, her teeth chattering.

He unbuckled his plaid and gave it to her. "Now ye maun try to get some rest," he ordered, and stretched out on the rock.

For some reason—the stony bed, the night's events, or

thoughts of the morrow—he could not sleep, and was almost relieved when he heard Kettie's whisper.

"What name might ye be called by?"

"Ross McCrae," he said shortly.

"It has a brave ring. Is your hame far distant?"

"Clear across Scotland and well to the north." For a minute he could see Loch Ruich's clear waters ringed by wooded hills. He could even see himself returning to Kindonal, piping a march of victory while the castle folk cried out a welcome.

"What o' your parents?" asked Kettie.

"My mother died when I was a babe," he said. "The Laird, being childless, raised me like his ain." He paused and added, "My father is piper to the clan."

No need to mention the shame he felt when folk whispered behind their hands that he was the son of the Laird's poor dead cousin, her who ran off with a piper when she could have made a proper match. That Black Donald still tuned his bagpipes in Kindonal Castle and marched at the head of the clan was a weakness on the Laird's part, said gossips. But Ross wondered if perhaps his father's enemies were merely jealous of his fame and skill in piping and his rugged good looks.

"I've not a soul to care for me," said Kettie wistfully.

"Ye'll have Mistress Seton's nurse," said Ross, yawning. The girl was quiet, and in a few minutes her soft breathing told him she was asleep.

Kettie's
Dream

Soon Ross too dozed off. How long he slept he could not tell. A muffled scream aroused him.

He jerked awake in the gray dawn. "Be still!" he muttered. "Do ye want them to find us?"

Kettie was huddled in his plaid, one hand to her mouth, her dark eyes wide in fear. "I could see ye," she blurted, "as clear as ye are now. 'Twas a fearful dream."

Her fright was contagious. Ross tried to laugh as he asked, "And was I on the castle wall with the captain? Or falling off the cliff with ye?"

"Far worse. Ye were in the midst of battle with the dead and dying all around. I could smell the blood and hear the cries." She put her hands over her ears.

Himself in the midst of battle? Perhaps she had indeed the gift of foresight. Doubt gnawed at him now as it did each time he raised his claymore, the two-edged Highland sword, in a practice drill. "Did I fight bravely?" he asked.

Her eyes widened. "I couldna tell. The dream changed.

I saw ye again, and ye were on a ship wi' other men sailing awa' across the ocean."

The girl must be daft. He had no mind to go to sea. Kettie's dreams could be no more than the nightmares every person had at one time or another.

"Ye're o'erwrought from last night's chase," he said. Partly to take her mind off her troubles, partly to steady his own nerves, he drew the chanter from his bagpipes and put it to his lips. Detached from the bag and drones, it produced a flutelike sound that would not be heard at any distance.

A gay little tune he had in mind, one that he had heard his father play in a lighthearted moment. He blew into the slender tube, his fingers remembering their places as the song came softly to life.

In some uncanny way the music changed between his mind's intent and the notes that came forth. Perhaps it was the fault of wind and wave, soughing and swishing. Perhaps because he had only the chanter on which to play. But in some way beyond his power, the song was not the merry lilt he had hoped for, but an eerie, haunting melody.

For a few minutes he kept on. No instrument could thwart him. But the sorrowful keening continued.

Disgusted, Ross slid the chanter into his belt, and noticed that the light had become stronger. Standing up, he stretched, and squinted at the cliff above. "Come alang," he said to the girl, and jumped down from the boulder.

They found a rough path up the cliff, and by clinging

to stone outcroppings, climbed to the top. Beyond, the land rose in a slow and steady sweep. All was gray and desolate, with only a faint glow lighting the sky.

They had not gone far beyond the cliffs when a furry form raced through the misty light, barking in joy. "Tam!" Ross knelt at the dog's side and threw his arms around him, while the animal lapped at his face and whined in delight.

Then Ross saw that Kettie had retreated to a distance and was cowering. "Will he bite?" she asked fearfully.

"Not unless I tell him to," said Ross. "Come ye here and gie him a pat."

But Kettie would not move. Finally Ross went up to her, Tam at his side, and forced her hand onto Tam's head. The dog twisted around, sniffed at her fingers, and then licked them in approval.

Kettie gave a cry of pleasure. "He likes me!" Timorously she patted the smooth fur.

Together the three set out, keeping close to some hawthorne hedgerows, and swinging wide to the south to avoid Tantallon. With luck they would not be sighted from the castle.

At a steady pace they continued through the glory of sunrise. By full daylight the land had come alive. Shepherds gathered flocks to drive them into the hills. Farmers scattered dry straw in the fields and set fire to the ripening barley and oats, in order that their grain could not be used by the advancing English army.

The road was filled with people. Women with bundles

over their shoulders, leading children by the hand, hastened to the towns for safety, some to North Berwick and some to Dunbar. Old men wheeled barrows of provisions. And a few stout fellows armed with pikes or claymores hurried to Edinburgh. No one paid any attention to the young Highlander with a dog and a girl. All were too concerned with their own troubles, set off by the beacons that had flared in the night.

At a cottage in the fold of the hills, Ross bought two loaves and some cheese. Farther on he and Kettie came to a ravine cut by a burbling brook.

"Shall we break our fast by yon burn?" Ross asked. He could hardly wait to taste the fragrant loaf. He was kneeling down, scooping up water in his hands and drinking thirstily, when he heard Kettie give a low cry of pleasure.

"Look!" she said. "Wild strawberries!"

While Ross cut the loaves and cheese with his dirk Kettie gathered some of the juicy red berries. A few minutes later she offered Ross a handful and began picking more for herself. Then she sat down near him and accepted gratefully the bread and cheese he held out to her.

The ravine offered shelter from the sea breeze; the sun shone warmly. Ross stretched out on the bank. The bread and cheese had satisfied his hunger; the taste of the berries was still sweet in his mouth.

Kettie sat a few feet away, Tam curled beside her. She was feeding him bits of her loaf. When he licked her hand in gratitude, she stroked his head fondly. For a girl who had been mortally afraid of dogs a few hours ago, she had certainly changed.

In a high sweet voice Kettie began to sing. Ross closed his eyes, listening to the ballad.

> *There were two sisters sat in a bower;*
> *Binnorie, O Binnorie.*
> *There came a knight to be their wooer*
> *By the bonny mill-dams of Binnorie.*
>
> *He courted the eldest wi' glove an' ring.*
> *Binnorie, O Binnorie,*
> *But he loved the youngest above a' thing*
> *By the bonny mill-dams of Binnorie.*

The tune was one that Ross knew well. He slipped the chanter from his belt, put it to his lips, and blew into it softly. Kettie's eyes lit up with pleasure as she continued her song.

> *The eldest she was vexed sair,*
> *Binnorie, O Binnorie,*
> *And much envied her sister fair*
> *By the bonny mill-dams of Binnorie.*

Together Kettie and Ross went through the entire ballad with its tale of the drowning of the younger girl, the harper's taking strands of her hair to string his harp, and the songs he played thereon.

The lasten tune that he played then,
Binnorie, O Binnorie,
Was woe to my sister, fair Ellen,
By the bonny mill-dams of Binnorie.

When the final plaintive note had died away, Ross shook out his chanter and started up guiltily. For a few minutes he had completely forgotten that he was on a mission for General Leslie and that the English were even now marching into Scotland.

"Come alang," he ordered impatiently.

By midday they had covered the dozen miles to the shepherd's hut, having skirted about the town of Dunbar. Ross had no trouble finding the cottage. It was set in a hollow beside the Broxburn, a short distance from where the stream crossed the Great Road on its way to the sea. The burn carved a deep gully along the foot of the high hill that rose from its southern bank; Doon Hill it was called.

The old nurse sat in her doorway spinning. Suspicious at first, she melted at sight of the brooch, and held out her arms to Kettie. "Welcome ye are to bide here. Me man's gone to the hills with the sheep, but I'll no' leave me hame for any Sassenachs, e'en though they be led by Cromwell."

Ross turned away, whistling Tam to his side. Now that

the nurse had taken charge of the girl, he could hurry north to Edinburgh, deliver his report, and rejoin his comrades.

He had gone only a few paces when Kettie ran up behind him. Snatching his hand, she bent and pressed her lips to it.

"I canna gie ye proper thanks," she said. "Ye hae saved my life and I'll ne'er forget. God willing, I may be o' help to ye one day."

Ross pulled his fingers away impatiently. "Dinna fash yersel' o'er me," he said. "An' forget about yer dreams. They're naught but fancies."

Kettie opened her mouth to speak, then closed it and curved her lips in a wan attempt at a smile. Ross turned abruptly and strode off. But for many a mile the memory of her pathetic face swam between him and the road.

Edinburgh

Ross walked until late afternoon, then climbed onto a cart laden with cheese and dried fish.

The driver, leather-faced and stooped, said, "Aye. I'm drivin' the beasts till I get me victuals well inside Edinburgh and the siller safe in me pocket. I'll not chance me stores being stole by the English."

"Could ye spare me a bite?" asked Ross, offering a coin. The driver produced oatcakes and a stone bottle of ale. Refreshed, Ross stretched out on the load, a large circular cheese at his head and a pile of fish at his back. In a few minutes Tam leaped up beside him. Ross hardly felt the jolting of the wheels on the rutted road and did not waken until twilight, when a sentry near Leith shouted a challenge.

At the outskirts of the city Ross jumped to the ground, calling out his thanks to the driver. Then he made his way through the thickly packed camp.

It was still a marvel to him that the Scottish army was composed of so many different elements. There were hard-bitten mercenaries, returned from Europe, who carried themselves as if they alone had any knowledge of war. There were Lowland levies, called to arms recently, and the regular Lowland regiments of the standing army. And there were Highland regiments and Highland levies like himself and others of his clan who had followed the Laird's call to arms.

Above the massed tents flew many-hued flags, their bright colors as varied as their devices. Some were narrow, some broad, and some swallow-tailed. Far off in the distance rose the insignia of the royal banner, the lion rampant in gold on the shield of Scotland. Ross wondered what the young King Charles was thinking now. Was he jubilant at the prospect of battle? Or did he, like Ross, harbor secret doubts as to his own prowess?

As Ross approached the Laird's tent, he passed a stocky man audibly engaged in evening devotions. Lachlan Maclachlan, the weaver, would not think of kneeling in prayer, such subservient posture being too reminiscent of popery for a strict Presbyterian.

" 'I will even appoint over you terror, consumption, and the burning ague, that shall consume the eyes and cause sorrow of heart.' " Lachlan's voice did not waver as Ross went by.

Near the entrance of the Laird's tent, Hugh MacPherson was crouched over a small fire. At Ross's step he rose. With his fair hair and slight figure, he looked little more than a lad, although he was two years Ross's senior and a married man. The Laird's clerk, he was forever penning notes to his dear Jeannie and wee bairn in the time between writing official messages.

"Has the Laird kept ye working late tonight?" Ross asked.

"Nay, he's sore ill," Hugh said. "Fair shakin' himself apart with a chill."

"The ague again," Ross said. "I thocht as much when I heard Lachlan's choice of Scripture. Hark ye, he's still at it."

" 'If thou wilt not observe to do all the words of this law that are written in this book,' " came Lachlan's voice, heavy with warning, " 'then the Lord will make all thy plagues wonderful.' "

Hugh sighed. "Lachlan is afraid that the Laird is too worldly."

"Would that he might find a more hopeful verse," Ross said. "The last time the Laird was taken ill he feared he'd not recover. I'll go in to him." Ague or not, the Laird, as his commanding officer, was the one to whom he must deliver the tally.

"Take this wi' ye and see if ye can get him to sup a bit." Hugh handed Ross a cup of heated wine.

The Laird was stretched out on a pallet, a blanket pulled to his chin. His sharp-featured face was white in the candlelight, his jutting nose and hooded eyes giving him the look of an aging falcon. Tremors shook his body.

Ross knelt down and put one arm under the older man's

head, lifted it, then held the cup to his lips. The Laird swallowed weakly and sank back.

"Ah, lad, ye're back. Did ye get to Tantallon?" So faint was his voice that Ross had to strain to hear it.

"Aye, and a fine fortress it is, as solid as the rock it stands on."

"And ye got the tally for Leslie?"

" 'Tis here." Ross drew out the folded paper. "Shall I read it to ye?"

The Laird's eyelids drooped. "Nay. Ye maun deliver it to the general." A spasm contorted his face.

Suddenly Ross was aware of his deep love for the Laird. Only to him had the older man revealed the tenderness that lay beneath his flinty exterior. "Are ye in pain?" he asked. "I'll fetch a surgeon."

"One came this morning." The words were very low. "I was better off before he bled me."

"Is there no way I can help ye?" Ross asked. He had never felt more helpless in his life.

"Nay. Get ye to Leslie." The Laird looked full at Ross, and in that instant he saw the shadow in the stern eyes.

Ross pressed the veined hand in farewell, not trusting himself to speak. Outside he handed the cup to Hugh, and whistled Tam to his side. Then he set out, now and then lifting a hand in greeting to fellow clansmen as he went. He almost stopped beside Duncan Muir, stretched out beside a small fire. Though Duncan did not hold a command post, he could no more help being a natural leader than he could help being over six feet and brawny as a giant. At home the villagers waited always for him to voice an opinion or to act. Invariably their actions and opinions mirrored his. Was Duncan aware of how seriously ill the Laird was? But Duncan was deep in conversation with John Davison, the schoolmaster who had recently come to Kindonal, so Ross continued on his way.

Farther on he heard the squawling notes of bagpipes as players filled their sheepskins. Inside a cluster of men stood his father and two other pipers. Black Donald towered above the rest, his head high, his handsome face flushed.

"Ho, lad," he called out. "Ye're just in time to aid me in upholdin' the honor of Kindonal. Bring out yer pipes and we'll show these McLeans how a pibroch should rightly be played."

Ross could hardly believe his ears. His father must think his playing had really improved! He started to reach for his pipes. Then he knew he must refuse.

"I canna stop now," he faltered. "I'm carryin' a message to the general."

Black Donald towered over Ross. "Is a wee paper to come before a father's wish, and the honor of the clan?" he thundered, liquor strong upon his breath. Pipers were deep drinkers, as everyone knew. Something about the blowing gave a man a powerful thirst, his father had explained.

"The Laird told me to deliver it tonight," maintained Ross. Didn't his father realize that the English had crossed the border?

"And who is closer to ye, the Laird or the man whose blood runs in yer body?" demanded the piper.

Ross put one hand on his father's arm. "There's naught I'd rather do than play the pibroch wi' ye, and I'm honored that ye ask. But this message may be o' import to General Leslie, so I maunna tarry."

As Ross sped away with Tam close at his heels he could hear his father's pipes snarling an angry protest. Not alone for his dark hair and beard had Black Donald earned his name. Yet Ross could not help but marvel at the skill with which he could make the bagpipes sing out his every mood, from high excitement to dark gloom. Of late his music had been mainly of storm and strife.

Near Calton Hill a sentry bristling with weapons challenged Ross. He strode forward into streets full of movement, glad that previous trips with the Laird had acquainted him with the layout of the city.

Lights gleamed from the Palace of Holyroodhouse. Across the way at the White Horse Inn more lights shone, and from the open door and windows issued bursts of excited talk. All along the road called the Canongate there was a constant movement of people outside the great houses of the nobility. Men hurried here and there preceded by lackeys carrying torches. Grooms with horses waited at doorways.

Up into High Street Ross hastened, past the shadowy Church of St. Giles and the gloomy prison, the Tolbooth, where a lone torch at the gate cast an eerie light on the

severed head of Montrose. Thank God the Earl's execution
and dismemberment had taken place in May, before Ross
had first reached Edinburgh, and that he had escaped
having to watch the spectacle. It had been bad enough standing guard at the burning of a witch a fortnight past. He put
his hand out and touched Tam's rough coat for reassurance.

Ross continued his climb, reached the heights of Castle
Hill, and crossed the moat to the castle's portcullis gate. In
the courtyard a troop of cavalry waited, the horses' hoofs
ringing sharply on the paving stones. Past one guard after
another Ross made his way upward, each time explaining
his errand, until he reached the Crown Square. Here activity had reached a fevered pitch. Officers and soldiers
moved in and out of the buildings that stood on each side
of the quadrangle.

On the steps of the Parliament Hall Ross was challenged
by a brusque red-faced man in a buff coat and tartan trews,
who took the inventory thankfully. "The meeting has just
finished. I'll give this to the general as he comes out. Wait
ye here in case he wants to question ye."

The great doors opened, guards clicked to attention, and
a group of men surged out, at their head a bent, crooked,
gray-haired man. Ross recognized General David Leslie,
commander in chief of the Army of the Covenant. Men
said that what he lacked in physical strength he more than
made up for by his skill in military administration, learned
in the hard school of the continental wars.

The general unfolded the tally, ran his eye over the contents, and spoke to the man in the buff coat. At his bidding Ross drew near.

"This lists the men and munitions," Leslie said in a dry voice. "What of Tantallon itself? Are the walls in good repair?"

Ross paused, recalling the various parts of the castle's battlements. He could not remember one piece of stonework that had crumbled.

"As solid as any I've seen," Ross said.

"What one man builds, another devises a means to destroy," said Leslie dourly. He turned away, and Ross knew that he was dismissed.

Down the castle's curving stone roadway he retraced his steps, between steep walls lit by flaring torches, out under the portcullis gate and across the broad courtyard. Then down the Lawnmarket, the High Street, and through the Nether Bow Port in the city wall.

Just beyond its archway, in the Canongate, a low wagon stood at the side of the causeway. A man toasted meat pasties over an iron pot filled with glowing coals. Ringed about him were a group of soldiers.

"Hot meat pies! Who'll hae one o' my nice hot pies?" the man cried.

The fragrance of pastry and spicy meat was tantalizing. Suddenly Ross was ravenous. He felt for a coin and joined the circle. "I'll take one," he called out.

The man next to him, heavy-set and brown-haired, turned his head. His mouth was crammed full, and flakes of

crust were on his lips. Trust Dougal MacFarlane to have
scented out any tasty treat. Even as a boy in Kindonal he
had loved good food above all else.

For a few moments Dougal could do nothing but chew.
Then he gave a mighty swallow and said, "We'd best eat
hearty tonight. The word is that we go out tomorrow to
meet Cromwell."

Tomorrow! So that was the reason for all the activity in
the city. A thrill of excitement—or was it dread?—shot
through Ross. Tomorrow he would know for certain
whether or not he could swing his claymore in a mortal
blow. The McCrae arms bore an upraised hand grasping a
sword with the word *Fortitudine* across it. Could he live up
to the line's tradition and fight bravely?

The vendor was holding a crisp pasty toward Ross. He
dug into his sporran, the small leather bag hung from his
waist, for a penny, took the pie, and sank his teeth into its
succulent richness. Beside him Tam gave a plaintive whine.
Ross handed the vendor another penny, and tossed the
pasty to the collie. A hasty gulp, and the meat pie was
half gone; another gulp, and it had disappeared.

Later Ross and Dougal returned together to camp. Only
a few fires glowed in the darkness, and the sentries' chal-
lenges were low-voiced. At the Laird's tent all was quiet.
Hugh slept soundly just outside the entrance. And the
Laird tossed in fitful slumber.

Ross wrapped himself in his plaid and, with Tam at his
back, settled himself at the Laird's feet, tormented by a

nameless fear. The ague is nothing new, he told himself. The Laird had been plagued with it for years. Still he could not erase from his mind the strange shadow he had detected in the old man's eyes.

For King and Covenant

Not the next day, nor the one after, nor the one following did Ross find his mettle put to the test on the field of battle. He and his fellow clansmen formed part of the force that General Leslie posted between the port of Leith and the city of Edinburgh to form a line of defense across the entrance to the heart of Scotland. With Scottish fortifications on Calton Hill and Arthur's Seat, the high promontories overlooking the city, it was no wonder that Cromwell did not attempt an attack.

Word of the English army's movements filtered through the Scottish camp. Cromwell had spent two days at Mordington, just over the Border, then marched on to Cockburnspath and to Dunbar, where his forces received supplies by ship from England.

Ross thought of Kettie in the shepherd's hut near the Great Road, the very route the English had taken. Had Kettie and the nurse taken flight, fearing the rumored brutality of the English? Or had they believed the promises of the proclamations that Cromwell had had posted in the market squares? One of them had been brought to camp and passed around among the Scots.

The paper, addressed to the people of Scotland, declared that in Charles Stuart and his party there could be no salvation, that Cromwell and his men sought the real substance of the Covenant, and that it would go "against their hearts to hurt a hair of any sincere servant of God."

Ross wondered if any armed force could be trusted to abide by such a statement in time of war.

That night after a meal of peas and fish and oatcakes, the Kindonal men discussed the proclamation around their fire. Tam was stretched out at Ross's feet.

Dougal MacFarlane scratched his head with a grimy forefinger. "All this talk about King and Covenant fair muddles me brain," he complained.

"I ken that we're in arms now for young King Charles and the Covenant," Ross said, "but I'm not certain of all that has gone before."

" 'Tis a muddling business," Duncan Muir agreed. "Even Leslie's regulars find it a puzzle why they should be fighting against Cromwell now, when six years ago at Marston Moor they stood shoulder to shoulder with his men."

John Davison looked up, his thin face and gray hair lit by the fire's glow. "I'm older than the rest of ye, and I can recall every step. Ye might say this present trouble began o'er ten years past, when King Charles decided he wanted the Scots to worship in his kirk with his bishops ruling us as they did the English."

Ross did know about that. Hadn't he been brought up on the tale of Jenny Geddes flinging her stool at the head of the minister in St. Giles when he read for the first time the hated English service?

" 'Twas then," continued Davison, "that the Scots drew up the National Covenant for the defense of Presbyterianism against Episcopacy and sent it throughout all o' Scotland for the signatures of the people. When Charles heard o' this defiance o' his authority, he marched against Scotland. But our soldiers met him at the border and drove him back. And he was forced to come to terms with us. Only Charles didna keep his word and went against his agreement, so a year or so later our army marched south across the border. That time the Scots stayed in the north of England till the English accepted our kirk."

"Me head's fair spinnin'." Dougal complained.

"Be quiet and ye might learn something," Ross said.

Davison went on, "Then Parliament took away so much of King Charles's power that he thought to gain it back by fighting. Since he had not enow power to raise an army in England, he came to Scotland and tried to form a Scottish force. But he got nowhere—only one man would listen to him, and that was the Earl of Montrose."

"May God rest his soul!" said Duncan Muir with a deep sigh.

Ross thought of the head on the Tolbooth gate, and felt a stab of pity. Although Montrose's enemies among the Covenanters had recently declared him a traitor and had brought about his execution, many Scots deemed the Earl a man of honor who had died for his loyalty to his sovereign.

"The English were fighting betwixt themselves; the whole country was torn by civil war. One side wanted Parliament to have power; the other held out for the king. When the first were near defeat, they cried out to Scotland for help, just as the king himself had. But not until Parliament signed our Solemn League and Covenant would we send an army into England to oppose the king. By this pledge Parliament agreed to preserve the Presbyterian religion in England, Scotland, and Ireland."

Ross had been but a lad when the Covenant was signed, but he remembered it well. The Laird had procured a copy of the document and had himself gone over it with Ross, making him read each word aloud. He could recall the scene as if it were yesterday, the Laird and himself at the long table in the Great Hall. He had been sleepy and had begged to be excused.

"Nay," the Laird had said, "the words will mean much in your lifetime. Ye maun listen, and ye maun remember the Covenant."

"After the signing of the Covenant," Davison continued, "came the battle of Marston Moor, when Scots and Parliament's forces fought side by side. After Cromwell was wounded, Alexander Leslie saved the day by ordering the

Scots cavalry against the Cavaliers. Aye, we saved Cromwell's skin that day!"

"But why be we against Cromwell now?" Dougal asked.

"Mainly because of religion," Duncan Muir said bitterly. "If I had my way, religion could go to. . . ." He broke off at Davison's warning glance.

"With all the fighting in England, the army opposing the king grew stronger and stronger, until it was the army and not Parliament that had the real power. And the leaders of the army had no mind to keep the Covenant. They were against having Presbyterianism as the only religion in the land, Cromwell and his soldiers being Independents," said Davison.

"What might be an Independent?" Dougal demanded.

"A man who wants to worship as he likes," Davison said shortly. "There's a lot more to it than that, but that's enow for this nicht. In any case, our quarrel with Cromwell, a good part of it, is over this question of religion. But a good part of it too has to do with the execution of the king."

Ross remembered it well. A little over a year ago Charles I had met death in London by the headsman's ax. His son, Charles Stuart, here this very night with Leslie's army, was recognized as sovereign only by the Scots.

"They had no right to cut off King Charles's head," said Dougal. "A king is a king; he's no' like common folk."

"Most of Scotland felt that way," Davison said. "That's why, now that Charles Stuart has signed the Covenant, we look upon him as King of Scotland."

"Aye, and we'll make him King of England, too!" boomed the hearty voice of Black Donald as he joined the group.

Ross looked at his father expectantly. Would he ask him now to practice a part of the pibroch? The next moment Black Donald spoke again, and Ross's spirits sank.

"Would some o' ye like to come on a foragin' sally wi' me? I hear there's a pedlar wi' a stock of usquebaugh no' far down the line."

Davison turned away. "Not I," he said. It was hard on a former schoolmaster to be interrupted in the midst of a lesson. Moreover, he had never developed a taste for whiskey, thinking it dulled the wits.

Dougal was on his feet. "I'll gae wi' ye, Donald," he said eagerly. "Think ye there might be a bite to eat, too?"

"I might as well join ye," rumbled Duncan Muir. "Though dinna expect me to match ye swallow for swallow."

Ross was starting to his feet to join the others when Black Donald turned on his heel. "A fine trio we'll make," he said. "Now let's awa'!"

The
Ravens

Ross sank back beside the fire, too hurt to move. His father had not acknowledged his presence by word or glance. Ross had thought all that was behind him. During his boyhood Black Donald had ignored him thus, paying him no more heed than one of the Laird's servant lads, or gillies.

Not until a year ago had his father so much as spoken to him. Ross had been walking alone one day beside Loch Ruich when Black Donald suddenly appeared and said abruptly, "That ye're the verra spit and image o' me I'll no' deny. But that ye hae our line's skill wi' the pipes, ye hae yet to prove. 'Tis time ye learned the feel o' the chanter."

Fiercely he had extended the bagpipes, and Ross had blown air into the sheepskin and tuned the drones as directed. But when he pressed air from the bag, his fingers on the chanter, he had managed only a few weak notes. His father had laughed raucously. "What good is yer book learnin' if ye canna pipe as yer grandsirs did?"

Ross had tried again, and a short while later he knew that he would never be satisfied until he had mastered the instrument. Suddenly it seemed very important that he be able to play tunes both merry and mournful, but chiefly the martial music that set men's minds and hearts afire.

From that time on Black Donald had taught Ross some of the skills that had been handed on from father to son for seven generations. He was a moody, exacting teacher, but Ross welcomed the lessons, not only because they satisfied his thirst for music but because they offered him a chance to become acquainted with his father. It was not long before he learned that Black Donald had never ceased grieving for the gentle girl who had died in Ross's infancy. Knowing that, Ross could forgive him his tempestuous outbursts.

There were other things his father confided in him, too. "Och, 'tis a strang weird that is laid on a piper. He canna gie in to his ain sorrow, but maun e'er lift up the spirits o' the clan." Black Donald's tone was grave. "Many is the nicht when the Laird and our men hae sat doleful about the fire that the need has come o'er me to pipe out demons that plagued 'em—demons of fear and despair that hung in the blackness. There was need to pipe new heart into 'em, too, that in the morn they might rise up wi' new strength and courage."

Black Donald ran a lean finger over the polished drones. "An' that is the reason I maun gie ye the same teachin' on the bagpipes that I had frae me father. 'Tis not just the

64

notes ye maun learn. 'Tis the reachin' down deep in yer ain soul to gie ithers the spirit they may hae forgot."

Ross had made no secret of his desire to play the bagpipes, and the Laird had put no obstacle in his way. Only once, with the arrival of the call to join the Army of the Covenant. Then he had said to Ross, "I had hoped ye might remain here at Kindonal to carry on till my return."

Black Donald had stormed, "I've watched ye make a milksop of me son. And now ye'd deny him the right to march wi' the clan!"

A milksop, was he? Ross had burned with anger. "I'll not stay behind. I'll go to battle!" he had declared. And here he was. He had thought of war as a swift strike upon the enemy, a time for bravery and courage. So far he had seen only long delays and no action.

Staring into the fire, Ross thought he had never felt more lonely in his life. He patted Tam's smooth head, thankful for the collie's presence. Most of his evenings since leaving Kindonal he had spent with the Laird and Hugh. But now they were in camp close to Edinburgh, the Laird being too ill to move with his men, and Hugh, as his aide, remaining with him.

Has the Laird recovered from the chills and fever? Ross wondered. He had hated to go off and leave the sick man, but he had been ordered to join the force that formed the line of defense. Just this morning he had seen two ravens quartering the sky over the Laird's camp. He had looked away, trying to convince himself that they were merely hunting. But he could not shake off the supposed significance of such a flight—an omen of death.

The fire had nearly gone out, and a chill was in the air. There's no point in brooding here, Ross thought. He might as well get out his pipes and practice the new march.

Usually the mere act of blowing air into the sheepskin gave him a feeling of excitement. Tonight he felt no rise of spirits, but doggedly set the bag under his arm, the blowpipe to his lips, and his fingers at their places on the chanter.

The first notes squealed forth uncertainly. Ross gripped the bag firmly with his elbow and blew gustily into the mouthpiece. He was not Black Donald's son for nothing. He must possess some fragment of his father's skill.

Determinedly he stepped out, matching his pace to the notes. The drones pointed skyward over his shoulder, and the brave tones of the march soared through the air. Louder and faster he played, gaining confidence with each rippling skirl. Finally the march ended in a triumphant burst of sound, and Ross halted, out of breath.

Only then did he notice that groups of men nearby had stopped their talk, and that John Davison had quit his pallet and stood with a smile on his lips.

"Ye've a braw touch wi' the pipes, lad," he said. "Fine enough to lead the clan to battle."

Ross shrugged. Small chance of that with Black Donald in his present mood.

Ross had freed the blowpipe and was shaking the moisture from it when he saw Hugh MacPherson hurrying toward him. Hugh's eyes were dark with shock and his face was distorted with grief.

"The Laird is dead!" he blurted.

The words sounded unreal in Ross's ears. For a moment he stood silent. The Laird had been father and mother to him when he was small, comforting his hurts, and visiting his bedside at night when he was ill with childhood ailments. He had taught Ross to read, his thin finger pointing to each letter in turn. During the past year he had taken Ross with him on brief journeys and had discussed clan matters with him as if training him for future leadership. Ross's mind could not encompass a world without the Laird's presence.

The following day the Laird's company of Highlanders were granted a brief leave from their posts of duty to accompany their leader to his grave. At the head of the clan were Black Donald and his son. Marching beside his father, his heart nearly bursting, Ross poured all his grief into the keening and wailing music. The sound rose in a torrent of anguish. Afterward, men said that rarely had Scotland heard a pibroch so moving and so sorrowful.

The
Trap

On the next day, the Sabbath, the English advanced from Haddington to Musselburgh, taking a stand about four miles from the Scottish army. All of Monday Ross and his companions waited in the pouring rain for the word to attack. The only command was for the line to stand fast, but word filtered through the ranks that a body of Cromwell's men had advanced toward the fortified hills and been driven off. Tuesday was swallowed up by continued waiting, as far as most of Leslie's men were concerned, although a troop of Scottish cavalry attacked the English rear guard as the enemy force returned to Musselburgh.

Huddled in a tent on the damp ground, the Kindonal men aired their views. Tam lay quiet beside Ross, his sharp nose resting on his paws.

"I didna march all this way to stand like a scarecrow in the rain," stormed Dougal.

"Nor I," Hugh said. "All I want is to get this o'er fast so I can get back to Jeannie and the babe."

"There are more ways o' fightin' than clashin' in combat," Duncan observed. "Think ye not that wet and hunger can weaken a force? We hae all of Scotland's stores behind us; the English hae naught but what they can bring in by ship."

"I say, gie us the chance to fight it out, man to man," blustered Black Donald. "I've yet to meet the Sassenach who can match this arm and blade." He drew his claymore and brandished it in the small space the tent afforded.

"I wouldna want to meet ye in battle," said John Davison quietly, "nor do I want to feel yer blade's bite now. I'll breathe easier when ye put it awa'."

Black Donald's blade rasped into its scabbard, and the talk continued. Suddenly trumpets sounded. Tam barked shrilly.

" 'Tis the signal to move!" Dougal cried.

But though all waited in hushed expectancy, no command came. In the distance bands of cavalry rode off.

"Maun we sit here forever?" Black Donald thundered.

His ire rose further when Davison observed mildly, "Just ye wait and see. Yon Leslie is a canny man."

"Canny at lettin' the English slip through his fingers," muttered the piper.

In the morning the cavalry returned, reporting some losses. The line of defense remained unbroken and unmoved.

During a week of storm and rain the Scots held their position. For all his secret doubts as to whether he could actually use his sword on a human being, Ross was becoming heartily sick of inaction. Almost anything would be better than this endless delay.

Then came word that the stormy weather had made impossible the landing of stores at Musselburgh, and so Cromwell had fallen back again to Dunbar.

Ross wondered anew about Kettie. How was she faring during the English occupation of Dunbar? Night after night her white face tormented him, and he wished he had thought of asking her to accompany him to Edinburgh.

All the rest of August month Ross and his companions held Leslie's line fast. The English marched here and there, tempting Leslie to come out from his strong position and do battle. But the Scottish general remained firmly entrenched.

It was a month of sorry weather and sour dispositions. There was extra work keeping rust from swords and muskets and trying to dry sodden clothes. But there was food enough to fill empty stomachs. And the English, so rumor said, were fast running out of supplies.

For himself, Ross would have liked fewer words and more action during the month. There had been more than enough words. Manifestoes from the invading English general and his officers to the Scots had begged them to lay aside their arms and listen to reason, insisting that the English were seeking the true substance of the Covenant and that both nations should work toward the same purpose. To this the General Assembly at Edinburgh made lengthy reply, which Cromwell answered in turn. Again there was a refutation of Cromwell's reply, and at length solemn declarations of intent to do battle.

On Saturday, the last day of August, the English were encamped just beyond the Scots, near Edinburgh. Before nightfall the English had burned the rude huts they had been occupying and had marched back toward Dunbar.

Ross was holding his damp plaid over a fire when he heard a distant command. In a few minutes came the order to form ranks.

Action at last! Ross flung the still steaming plaid over his shoulder and buckled it about his waist, his sporran at the front, his dirk at one side, and his claymore at the other. On his back he hung his targe, a round shield of wood and leather. Then he picked up his bagpipes and went to his father.

Black Donald stood waiting, his cheeks puffed as he blew air into his instrument. Then, his foot tapping impatiently, he grinned at Ross and said, "Shall we gie them a rouse, ye and I?"

Ross looked at the dark eyes afire with excitement and the brilliant smile. At that moment he would have followed his father anywhere.

In answer he lifted his blowpipe to his lips. No clan would have more stirring music; no piper would blow with more spirit. Today he would make Black Donald proud of his son.

They set off, the cry of the clan loud in their ears. "*Sgur Urain!*" came the shout, again and again. It was the name of a mountain in Kindonal where an early victory had taken place. Ross was confident that the battle in which they would soon be engaged would be a victory too.

But there was no battle that day. All through the night and the next day, which was the Sabbath and the first day of September, Leslie did no more than press close upon the rear of Cromwell's army.

Just outside of Dunbar the Scots swung to the south, around the English forces, and climbed the heights of Doon Hill. The rain was beating down in great gusts that night, and Ross could see little of the land around him as he fashioned a rude shelter from corn stalks. Tam was with him, having followed the clan on its march. The wet sheaves provided poor shelter, but with Tam warm at his back, Ross slept.

The next morning, even in the sweeping rain, he could tell that General Leslie had chosen a rare vantage point. From the long sweeping hillside Ross could see the English forces camped on the lowlands below, separated from the Scots by the Broxburn, the small stream in a deep ravine that edged the margin of Doon Hill. To the right was the Great Road to England, now in the control of the Scots, who could cut off any attempted English retreat along the highway to the border. And the Scots far outnumbered the English. There must be twenty-three thousand of Leslie's men spread out on the high slope of Doon Hill, and only

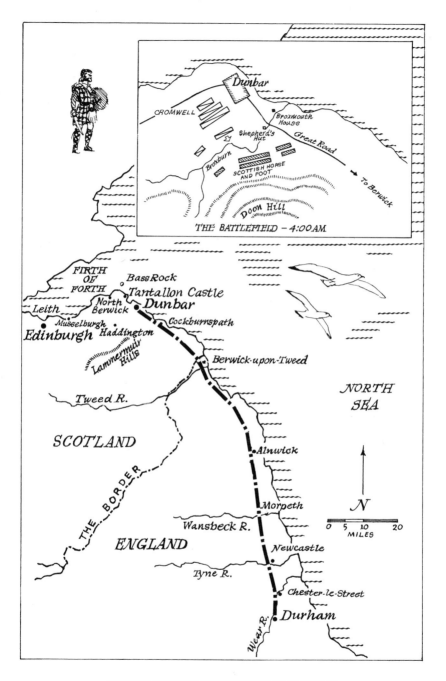

ROUTE OF THE SCOTS AFTER THE BATTLE OF DUNBAR

half as many with Cromwell encamped on the soggy plains. Surely Leslie had caught the English in a trap from which they could not escape.

Beyond the English force lay the dark roofs of Dunbar, and behind the town surged the North Sea, foaming with whitecaps and lashed by rain. Ross could smell the salt in the wet gusts that stung his face.

Far below on the bank of the Broxburn, near where it crossed the Great Road, Ross could make out the outlines of the hut where he had left Kettie. Now English troops occupied the low building.

That afternoon Tam ran barking to a small thicket. Following him, Ross found a small boy crouched miserably under a blackberry bush. "What might ye be about?" Ross inquired.

"I came but to see were there any brambles," the boy said, digging dirty fists into his eyes. "We Dunbar folk be sair empty."

The lad was no more than skin and bones. He must be telling the truth.

"If I had a bite, I'd share it wi' ye," Ross said. The last of the Scottish army stores had been distributed yesterday morning, a bare handful of meal to each man.

"Do ye ken the shepherd that lived in the hut on the Broxburn?" Ross asked.

"Aye," the boy answered guardedly.

"What befell his wife and the girl?"

The lad looked puzzled. "The boy, ye mean? He and

the old woman went into the town. They're lodged near the kirk."

"Do ye know aught of a girl that was wi' the dame?" Ross pressed. He had not seen a boy on the day he had left Kettie. Perhaps he had been in the hills with the sheep.

"Nay, there was no girl," stated the boy. Then he asked, "Will there be a battle?"

"That I canna tell," said Ross. "But ye had best get back the same way ye came, lest ye be harmed." He watched the boy dart into the thicket again, then disappear.

Tormented by thoughts of Kettie, he wondered if she had been taken ill. Or perhaps she had been discovered and forced to return to Tantallon. His mind shied away from the consequences of such a return. Where could she be if not with the old nurse? His mind went round and round like a bird seeking escape from a cage.

About four in the afternoon came the order for the artillery to move down Doon Hill toward the burn. There were grumblings and protests. Why was Leslie leaving so strong a vantage point? Soon the infantry was commanded to follow. By nightfall Ross waited with his company on the lower slopes of the hillside. On his right the cavalry moved with metallic clank and rattle toward the level ground near the pass of the Broxburn.

"Old Noll's headquarters are in Broxmouth House, I hear, just t'ither side o' the highway," volunteered Black Donald. "Leslie must be planning to send our cavalry to capture him i' the morn."

"Where did ye pick up that bit o' news?" Duncan asked.

"O'er a jug of usquebaugh, where else?" said the piper, laughing. "When officers get a thirst they're not above sharin' what they ken."

Ross whistled Tam to his side, wrapped up in his plaid, and settled himself under a bush. The rain was still falling, and the wind was whipping it about madly. He had almost forgotten what it was to be dry. But at midnight he must stand watch, and if he were to stay awake then he must try to snatch some sleep now. Tam pressed against his back. Soon they were both deep in slumber.

The
Attack

"Up, lad, to stand yer watch!"

Ross was roused by Duncan's hand on his shoulder. A shower of drops fell on him as he rose stiffly to his feet and clasped the damp folds of his plaid about his shivering frame. Tam pressed against his leg, and Ross patted the dog's rough coat.

A few feet away Black Donald slept heavily. Other men huddled in wakeful groups, talking in low voices.

"The time is nigh," said Duncan soberly. "Leslie will strike with the sunrise, or I'm much mistaken."

Ross stooped and picked up his claymore, the weight of the two-edged sword as heavy in his hand as the heaviness in his mind. He tried to shrug off his disquiet. Yesterday's rainstorm had been enough to down the spirits of any man. With daylight there would be battle and certain victory.

He left Duncan to settle down in the space he had quit, and with Tam by his side walked to the top of the hill. After reporting to the officer in charge, he began to tramp back and forth from his post to the next. It was good to walk. The movement stirred some semblance of warmth in his limbs.

The ground was wet and slippery, the grain and grass that covered the hillside having been trampled to a muddy mass in the movements of the past few days. The air, however, was clear. In the dark sky the clouds thinned now and then to reveal a faint glow from the partially obscured moon.

Here and there a man knelt in earnest exhortation to the Lord to make His faithful soldiers of the Covenant victorious in battle. To Ross's ears came the words: "Blessed be the Lord my strength, which teacheth my hands to war and my fingers to fight; my goodness and my fortress; my high tower and my deliverer; my shield and He in whom I trust."

Englishmen were probably sending up similar prayers from their side of the Broxburn, thought Ross. In all their proclamations and notices they made firm claim that they were fighting for the Lord of Hosts.

A chill breeze, remnant of the gale that had lashed the coast for days, blew against Ross's face. He studied the dark masses on the plain below where campfires dully glowed. Was he imagining it, or was there some movement in the enemy's left flank?

On his next turn, Ross spoke to the officer in command. "Hae ye noted that the English are moving toward the road?"

The man peered into the night. "They've been moving about for hours. What odds where they go? They've no place to march but out to sea."

A messenger approached. "Gie the order to extinguish all matches but two to a company," he said. "The supply is nigh exhausted."

Matches were cords used to fire the priming of match-lock guns. Later, just before the battle, the infantry could relight their matches. Flintlock guns were more practical, their spark being available on a moment's notice, but they were new and in short supply.

Ross passed along the order, then resumed his pacing. Of all the hours in the twenty-four, those from midnight until dawn seemed the longest. And the lowest. Then a man's spirit was at its ebb. Even his strength failed.

Resolutely Ross forced his flagging limbs to action. Back and forth he went, stopping and peering into the dark, turning and marching again, taking care all the time lest he slip. Beside him trotted Tam, close as a shadow.

Hours passed, and high in the sky the moon gleamed out from behind the clouds. A pale streak of dawn shone over the distant shore. Ross tensed. Soon Leslie would order a move.

Suddenly, far down to his right, a peal of trumpets sounded. There was a vast clanking of armor, the neighing of hundreds of horses, and a mighty shout, "The Lord of Hosts!"

The attack! It had come! And from the English!

Ross whirled to see the sleeping Scots come clumsily to life. Men who had been keeping their muskets dry under their plaids hastily unwrapped them. Those with match-locks ran about seeking a light from the too few whose matches had not been extinguished. Pikemen milled this way and that, hastily trying to form ranks. Gunners crawled from beneath their weapons to fumble with shot and charges. Everywhere was utter confusion.

Tam barked, and Ross grasped his thick ruff. A dog had no place in battle. Putting his face close to the animal's, Ross commanded firmly, "Begone!"

Not waiting to watch the collie run off out of sight, Ross hurried from his hilltop post, down past shouting, jostling men, to his own group. Where was his father? He should be rallying the clan. There he was, half under a shock of corn, and still sleeping amidst the din. In a frenzy Ross jerked him to his feet.

Wild-eyed, Black Donald gazed about. "Good God! A surprise attack!" He clutched at his bagpipes and frantically blew air into the sheepskin.

Ross snatched up his own pipes, tucked the bag under his arm, and started filling it with anguished speed. He was fingering the chanter when he heard a burst of notes beside him. His father was calling the clan to arms, the wild sounds tearing across the crowded turmoil with an eerie compulsion.

Ross joined his notes to his father's, his heart swelling with an almost unbearable excitement. Far down Doon Hill on the right wing near the highway came the thundering clash of metal on metal. Ross could make out a mass of English horsemen, a tumultuous wave of bristling weapons, pressing upon the Scottish cavalry. The two opposing forces surged together with a clanking of armor, the defiant cries of riders, and the shrill scream of horses. The onrushing steeds halted, then fell back. Ah! The English were beaten. Ross knew a thrill of triumph. Of course Leslie's men had prevailed. A moment later he stared in wonder. The English were riding forward again. And with wild battle cries the Scottish cavalry moved to clash with them.

Then the press of men cut off Ross's view. From all around him rose exultant shouts. "The Covenant! The Covenant!" Highlanders and Lowlanders roared their defiance.

Ross played on, caught up in fierce excitement. He and Black Donald moved down the hill, side by side, their bagpipes skirling madly in a brave rush of sound. Down they strode over wet grass and through mud, the clan pressing close behind.

Ahead other Scots were tightly massed on the steep banks of the gully, and beyond, across the brook, were arrayed the ranks of Cromwell's army.

Scottish officers shouted commands, striving to make themselves heard above the din. Close by, others roared countermanding orders. Leslie's forces churned in unutterable chaos.

Suddenly, on the English side of the gully, there were

flashes of fire from snaphances and matchlocks, bursts of smoke, and the thunder of fieldpieces as artillery and infantry fired into the milling Scots. Shot tore into the thickly gathered Scots. Ross heard shrieks of pain all around him.

Some men surged forward, others backward, tripping over the fallen and slain. Never in his blackest nightmares had Ross pictured such frightful pandemonium. His anguish was the greater that he could in no way retaliate, but could only stand helplessly while enemy bullets ripped through Scottish limbs.

In the stampede Ross's bagpipes were torn from his grasp, and he was pushed roughly to the ground. Struggling to his feet, he strained to catch a glimpse of his father but could not.

Ross wrenched his claymore free and held it ready, but surrounded as he was by his own countrymen, he dared not swing. He had never known such sickening, fearful frustration.

The English fire continued, wreaking havoc among Leslie's forces. It was answered by a few scattered bursts from the Scots. If only a thrifty officer had not given that fateful order to extinguish matches!

For what seemed a hellish eternity Ross struggled to move ahead. In front of him a man fell, clutching at his chest. Beyond, an officer was waving a sword in the air, urging his men forward, when a ball carried away his arm. Beside him a youth spun around with an unearthly screech, his belly ripped open. Above the sound of cannon rose the screams of men in agony.

Ross clung tightly to his sword. If only he could get near enough the enemy to use it. He must make at least one Englishman taste the brutal slaughter that was felling his comrades. He heard again the cry, "The Covenant!" and made another frenzied effort to force his way forward.

The ranks ahead opened for a moment, and he could see English pikemen descending the bank of the ravine, a fearsome array of pointed steel. Then they started up the Scots' side of the gully, a well-nigh impregnable force.

Ross tried to stand his ground. If he could strike one blow, just one blow for Scotland! Then there was a clamor from the right wing, and he was swept backward by a mighty surge of men and beasts in a hideous tangle of flying hoofs and broken, bleeding bodies. The English cavalry had broken through the Scottish horses and driven them down upon the foot regiments!

Ross could feel the press of bodies against his own as the infantry struggled to get out of the way of the advancing horses. Then the line of soldiers collapsed under the brunt of the cavalry. Men fell to be trampled underfoot. Mounts and riders alike were sheathed in metal, each a galloping arsenal of sharp edges and bared weapons that tore through the light garments of the foot soldiers and into their flesh and bone.

Frantic with fear, Ross tried to dodge the crazed beasts

that plunged and reared all about him. A horse clumsy with heavy armor stumbled above Ross. In terror he dropped his claymore to clasp the stirrup and swing himself out of the way. The steed's dead rider fell across Ross, and the horse plunged onward.

Ross tried to scramble to his feet, but was caught in a maelstrom. He tried to dodge an onrushing horse. Then he felt a mighty blow on his head, and knew no more.

Defeat

The chanting of a psalm aroused Ross. He opened his eyes. In one swift glance he could see enough to make him close them immediately.

Almost directly in front of where he lay, surrounded by the dead and dying, was a troop of horsemen, their blood-red shirts made livid by the first rays of the rising sun. At their head was a powerful man in cuirass and helmet, his strong-featured face raised to the sky. His nose was long and bulbous, his mouth broad, with a large mole under his lower lip, and his eyes were lit by exaltation as he led the troop in chanting:

> *Let God arise, and scattered*
> *Let all His enemies be;*
> *And let all those that do Him hate*
> *Before His presence flee!*
>
> *O give ye praise unto the Lord,*

All nations that be;
Likewise ye people all, accord
His name to magnify!

For great to-us-ward ever are
His loving kindnesses;
His truth endures forevermore:
The Lord O do ye bless!

The troopers repeated the verses in well-drilled unison. Ross opened his eyes a crack at the conclusion and saw that other horsemen were galloping up to their leader, wave after wave of them, like an onrushing tide. This man with the exalted air who sat so strongly at the head of the cavalry—this man must be Oliver Cromwell, commander in chief of all the English forces, *Ironsides* himself!

Then Cromwell lifted his arm and cried out, "The Lord God of Hosts!" With a rattle of swords and armor, and a jarring thud of hoofbeats, the cavalry rode off.

Ross sank again into unconsciousness. When he next revived, he tried to lift his head. It hurt ferociously, and his exploring fingers found a huge swelling over his temple where he had been dealt a heavy blow. He struggled to his feet and picked up a sword that lay nearby.

His head swimming, Ross looked at a scene of terrible carnage. The air was filled with the cries of the wounded, and the ground was littered with bodies. Some lay at grotesque angles, others moved feebly. In the distance the English cavalry galloped after a horde of horsemen and foot soldiers who ran in unutterable confusion.

Defeat. Utter rout. Surely this must be a nightmare. Ross stumbled along. Miraculously he had escaped death. And for the moment he was free. Somehow he must get away from the battlefield before the English returned from their pursuit of the rest of the Scottish army and took him prisoner. If he ran now, hiding in the hedgerows, he might with luck reach the wild parts of the Lammermuir Hills, then take a circuitous route to Tantallon Castle. In that fortress he would be safe from any attack.

Ross had taken a few steps when with a pang he remembered his father. Might he be among the fallen? His head reeling, Ross started to look among the bleeding bodies, some writhing, some stiff. Swiftly he scanned the bloodied faces, the distorted limbs. Not many Scots had Black Donald's height and breadth. If he lay nearby—and in the melee he could not have moved far—he should be easy to identify.

Breathlessly Ross searched, his ears filled with the piteous cries of the wounded. He had begun to think that his father must be among the routed soldiers fleeing the conquering host, when a sprawled form caught his eye.

Black Donald lay in a pool of blood, his head half severed from his shoulders, and tilted at a crazy angle. His dark eyes stared vacantly at the sky; his lips were curled back from his strong teeth. His bagpipes were caught under his arm.

Ross began to tremble and fell to his knees. He heard sobs and put a hand to his mouth. The sobbing was his own.

The staring eyes looked up at him. I must cover them, he thought, and he plucked at his father's plaid. The wool was blood-soaked and worn, not fit for a shroud.

Hardly knowing what he was doing, Ross unclasped the belt at his father's waist and pulled the threadbare woolen cloth away. As he turned the body, air that had been trapped in the bagpipes was released, emitting a high weird sound like a lament.

Shaking, Ross doffed his own plaid and wrapped his father's head and body in its folds. After he had fastened the belt about the bound corpse he looked around frantically. More than cloth would be needed if the body were not to be torn to pieces by preying birds or beasts.

Nearby was a trench with sodden ashes at the bottom. Men had dug it yesterday to shield their fire from the wind. Ross heaved and tugged at the wrapped corpse, and dragged it to the pit. The hole was too shallow for a proper grave, but it would have to serve.

He must cover the body now. With his bare hands he started to claw at the loose earth beside the pit, then picked up a shield beside a slain clansman a few feet away and used that to push dirt over the lifeless bundle. When he had finished, he stood shaking uncontrollably. Through chattering teeth he said, "Peace. Rest ye in peace."

Looking about, Ross saw that among the fallen there was scattered movement. Others like himself must have lost consciousness or feigned it, and now that the cavalry had moved on, were attempting to find some refuge from the avenging fury of Cromwell's army. No one expected the Roundheads to give quarter.

Ross picked up his father's worn plaid and bagpipes, wound them into an awkward bundle, and started up the slope. His numbed brain held only one thought—flight.

He had gone a few steps when he saw a burly figure attempting to rise. One arm hung helpless, dripping blood. It was Duncan Muir, with his sword arm slashed open. Ross made his way over prostrate bodies to his friend's side.

"Could I but rip a bit off my shirt," said Duncan, "I might stanch the flow."

At Ross's feet was a body with outflung limbs, the head crushed to a shapeless mass. This was no time to be squeamish. In frantic haste Ross tore a length from the dead man's saffron tunic and bound the cloth tight about Duncan's arm. The blood oozed through, but no longer streamed over the massive hand.

They set off together up the hillside. Ross stole a glance over his shoulder at the plain where the English infantry was swarming over the steep banks of the ravine.

"Make haste," urged Ross. "We may yet get awa'."

"We can gie it a try," muttered Duncan.

If the flattened grain were not so slippery, if the dizziness in my head were not so great and my legs not so reluctant to obey, I might have a chance, thought Ross. Behind him Duncan Muir panted hoarsely. His usually ruddy face had paled beneath his shock of sandy hair.

"Can we but reach the woods ahead," Ross gasped. He

forced his trembling legs toward a stand of trees on the side of the hill.

They were a few rods from the woods when a band of horsemen galloped from a fold of the hills. Ross reached for his claymore. He would go down fighting. But even as he raised it, the sword was struck from his grasp by a soldier on a dun horse. Ross staggered back, his hand numbed by the force of the stroke.

Tensed, he waited for the next swing of the horseman's blade. Its metal mirrored the sun's rays and dazzled him. A gruff voice shouted, "Stay your hand, Bruton. We're to capture not kill them."

The sword moved, and Ross could see the speaker, a slight dark man on a black horse.

"Capture? And to what end? There's only one way to keep a Scot from taking up arms again." The man called Bruton had a narrow face, twisted now in hatred.

"Orders from Cromwell himself," said the other. "Detail a guard to return these men to the field, and let's get on. There are hundreds yet on the loose."

Dimly Ross saw a soldier pick up his claymore. When a rough hand plucked the dirk from his belt, he fought down an impulse to resist. No one in his right mind would be fool enough to give the man on the dun horse an excuse to strike again. This time he might not stay his hand.

Suddenly the soldier snatched at the rolled-up plaid that Ross carried. "What might be in here?" he demanded, and whipped the bundle open.

The bagpipes fell to the ground. The soldier kicked at them. "Ye'll have no use for those where you're going," he said. Then he flung the empty plaid back to Ross.

Duncan Muir, standing at Ross's side, was swaying. His massive frame sagged. " 'Tis over," he said grimly, "for us all."

The Smugglers' Caves

Herded with thousands of other prisoners on the lower slopes of Doon Hill, Ross and Duncan waited side by side through the long hours of the morning and early afternoon.

Ross sat with his knees drawn up, his head resting on them. He had never known such a splitting pain in his head. When he moved he was nearly overcome by dizziness. And the gnawing ache in his middle was a reminder of his hunger. How long since he had last eaten a decent meal? Two days? Three? His throbbing head reeled with the effort of remembering.

Over the battlefield flocks of ravens rose and fell in ever increasing swarms. Ross turned his back on the sight. He had seen what ravens could do to a sheep, and he had no wish to watch what they might do to the dead, or worse yet, to the dying. There was some small comfort in the knowledge that his father's body was safe from the rapacious beaks.

A short distance away a voice said, " 'Wheresoever the

carcass is, there will the eagles be gathered together.' "
Surely those must be Lachlan's sententious tones. Ross
looked over his shoulder and saw the weaver. One hand
was clenched on his breast, and he was saying with an
agonized expression, " 'God hath delivered me to the un-
godly, and turned me over into the hands of the wicked.' "

When Lachlan lifted up his head, Ross waved and called
out. Lachlan gave a cry of recognition and made his way
toward Ross and Duncan.

"I thoucht I was the only ane from Kindonal who was
ta'en," he said.

"Only the Lord kens how many there be," said Duncan.

Lachlan lowered himself to the ground, and the three
sat in wordless misery.

Above and beneath Ross's physical pain was the agony
of his father's death. He thrust the memory away. It was
enough to accept the fact of defeat. He could not fathom
the mystery of it.

Yesterday the Scots had outnumbered the English nearly
two to one; they had the advantage in position as well as
numbers. Today they were a vanquished army. Hundreds
lay dead on the field; other hundreds lay wounded among
them. And all about was an ever increasing throng of
captives.

Some were Highland levies like himself, some were Lowland levies, but the greatest segment were those who formed
the main core of the regular army. He heard a man nearby
say that two hundred colors had been taken, the whole

baggage and trainband, and all the artillery, great and small, including thirty guns. The battle might well be called "Dunbar Rout." The voice went on to say that ten thousand Scots had been captured. Looking at the endless sea of bitter faces around him, Ross could believe that figure. But what of the others from Kindonal? Did Hugh and Dougal and John Davison still live? Or did they lie dead on the battlefield?

Of more immediate concern was the fate of the prisoners. Rumors ran about the crowded hillside. Cromwell would put them all to the sword. He would keep them here until they starved. Or he would send them south to England.

In the middle of the afternoon the mounted troopers that had been guarding the prisoners started forming the mass of Scots into a double file along the Great Road, facing them toward the south. Some horsemen rode at the head of the long column, others at the rear, while the majority were strung out along the line, one to every twenty prisoners.

"To England it is," muttered Duncan Muir. He wavered beside Ross, cradling his injured arm, his lips pressed tight in pain. Ross was silent. Of what use were words?

While waiting for an order to move, Ross studied two men just ahead in the line. One was thin, the other heavy-set, Lowlanders by their speech and native to the area.

"We'll be goin' by Cove Harbour, past me Annie's house," the slight one said.

"And by Margery's, too. Think ye they'll be lookin' out fer us?" the other asked.

"Likely they'll be hidin' in the cow stalls in the byre," the first said.

"Aye, or in the smugglers' caves."

"Would that we were there now!" the thin chap said wistfully.

"Och, aye!" The second man sighed gustily.

A horseman rode alongside, sword in hand, his spurs jangling. "March, you scum, march!" he ordered. Ross recognized Bruton, the man who had nearly run him through in the morning.

Trying not to jar his aching head, Ross walked stiffly forward. The straggling line moved slowly, urged on by the mounted guard. On either side were trampled fields, drying in the sun. Here and there a clump of daisies shone white and gold, and poppies gleamed scarlet. Laverocks sang and pewits swooped, as if this were any September afternoon, not the black day on which the Scottish army had met bitter defeat.

Now and then the long file passed a cottage. But though he scanned each small window with care, Ross could detect no sign of human habitation. What folk there were inside, if indeed there were any, must be cowering out of sight. The column had covered perhaps six miles when the two Lowlanders began talking again.

"Just around this next bend," said the slight one.

"I ne'er thought to go by Margery's house in so sorry a state," the other said mournfully.

They slogged on. Just ahead on the edge of a deep ravine, leading seaward, stood a cow barn, and on the other side of the road was a cottage. From its open doorway stepped two pretty girls in bright gowns, their hair decked with ribbons and flowers, their smiles welcoming.

"I canna believe me eyes!" the stocky man exclaimed. "Do ye see what I see?"

After miles of deserted roadside, the sight of the girls was enough to shock any loyal Scot. Ross watched sourly as Bruton and the nearest horseman rode up to the cottage and reined in.

"Would ye like some cakes and a bit of a drink?" one of the girls called out. Was Ross imagining it, or did her voice tremble?

"Would ye nae like to come in?" the other invited. Her cheeks were very red, and she kept her eyes fastened on the cavalrymen.

The prisoners in front of Ross had stopped in their tracks. One lifted his fist. "To think that my Annie would shine up to a Sassenach!" he said in disgust.

The other Lowlander grabbed his arm. "I'll not stand for it," he said. "Let's go for them. Better to be dead than witness to such shame."

Bruton leaned down toward the girls. "What of your sweethearts? Surely ladies as pretty as you have admirers."

"Those feckless gowks wouldna hae the wit to run when they had a chance." The first girl tossed her head.

"Why think on them? They're best gone." The second girl threw a frantic glance toward the two prisoners. Then she smiled up at the cavalrymen. "Will ye come in for a bite?"

The horsemen dismounted. Bruton gave the reins of his steed to a young guard. "Keep the horses here whilst we go in. We'll not be long." They followed the girls into the cottage, and the door closed. For the moment no other soldiers were in sight on the winding road.

The two Lowlanders were staring in fury at the cottage. While the guard's back was turned, Duncan urged softly, "Run, ye fools, whilst ye hae the chance. Ken ye not that the lasses hae done this for ye?"

One opened his mouth in amazement. "The caves!" he whispered.

The other stepped forward in sudden awareness. Then they both bent low, skimmed across the road, and ran behind the barn.

For one wild minute Ross thought of following. Then the guard turned, and the opportunity was lost.

A few seconds later another guard galloped up and kicked at the door of the cottage, bellowing in anger. The troopers boiled out, mounted in haste, and started the Scots in motion, not noticing that there were two fewer prisoners in line.

Before they rode off, Ross heard Bruton say, "Oatcakes and milk, sour at that. Pretty poor fare."

Ross tightened his belt. What he wouldn't give for just one sip of milk, sour or fresh. And as for an oatcake—he couldn't imagine anything finer. The mere thought of it made him ravenous. More from habit than expectation he felt in his sporran. The leather bag was empty, but his exploring fingers found a few oats in the seam. He put them in his mouth and rolled them around with his tongue. They were too scanty to chew.

At the ford near Pease Glen he scooped up some of the water from the burn. Although muddy from scores of feet, it was cool to his parched mouth.

The
Cliff

The wavering column crawled along. The Scots moved forward a few steps, then halted, inched on, then stopped again. Ross thought they might have gone a mile or so beyond Cove Harbour when they again came to a standstill. Soon they were ordered into an open field edged by a steep cliff overlooking the sea, and the guards took up positions on the landward side. Ross ventured to the brink of the precipice and peered over. Far below at the base of almost perpendicular rocks, the sea broke in foaming waves.

"The devil himself couldna pick a worse place for us to spend the nicht," groaned a man near Ross. "There's nae a mite of shelter frae the wind."

" 'Tis easy to see why they put us here," another commented. "They need watch only the landward side."

"I'll risk a climb down those cliffs come nightfall," ventured a third.

"More fool ye if ye do," said a fourth man. "I grew up no'

far from here, and I'd no' chance such a trip at noonday."

Ross hardly heard them. Escaping over the cliffs was out of the question for him. He was so giddy he could barely set one foot in front of the other. And Duncan's situation was no better, with one arm useless.

Numb with fatigue, Ross sank down on the heather. Overhead a large flock of gulls—more than he had ever seen together at one time—dipped and soared. Could it be true, as he had heard in childhood, that sea gulls were the spirits of men killed in battle, ever wary, ever on guard, the bright red spots on their beaks the symbol of their wounds? Might one of these birds be the spirit of Black Donald?

Gradually he became aware of the sky in sunset, a glory of gold and scarlet, tinting the steep shoreline and its scalloped bays, giving an unearthly beauty to the cliffs and purple hills. In the distance he could see Bass Rock and the conical shape of North Berwick Law. Far beyond were the Highlands. Would he ever see them again?

The brilliant colors were fading when Ross heard a dog barking. The throaty cry pierced through the fog of his despair. No, he told himself, it cannot be Tam.

The barking grew louder and rose to a frenzied yelping. Ross peered against the sunset. Then he saw a brown-and-black collie threading its way between the captives. Clinging to a frayed rope that encircled the dog's neck ran a slender youth, his short fair hair blowing back from his thin face.

In a moment the dog reached Ross and jumped up on

him, licking his cheek and whining in ecstasy. With a deep sigh the boy sank down on the ground and looked at Ross, great dark eyes brimming. Where had he seen those eyes before?

Suddenly he knew. "Kettie!" he blurted in disbelief. "What might ye be doin' here?"

"I had to find ye," she said, "so I followed Tam. I found him wanderin' about the streets of Dunbar."

When he sent Tam away, the dog must have gone to the town and recognized Kettie when he met her again. Her cropped hair and boy's attire could not deceive Tam's keen nostrils. Kettie must have guessed that he had been taken prisoner, and had let Tam lead her here.

She pressed a cloth bag into his hand. " 'Tis not much, but 'tis all I could find."

There were oats in the bag. "You shouldna—" he began, then he was silent. This was no time to be proud. "Thank ye," he muttered, noting how sharply her bones showed through her clothes.

"And here be yer bagpipes," she said, holding the instrument out to him.

His pipes! "Where did ye get these?" Ross demanded.

"The fighting was scarce o'er when I came across Tam, as fearful a dog as e'er I've seen," said Kettie. "Later in the day the English soldiers told the Dunbar folk they might carry off those too sorely wounded to walk. When I went to the battlefield Tam came with me."

"*You* went *there?*" How could a delicate, sensitive girl bear the horror of a battlefield?

"I was looking for ye," Kettie said simply.

Ross turned his eyes away from hers. He was not worthy of such devotion.

"Tam found your bagpipes, and then he led me alang the road until he found ye," she finished.

"It was good of ye to bring me the pipes," he said, "but ye maun haste back to Dunbar. 'Tis not safe for ye to be abroad."

The next minute his fears for Kettie were realized. There was a jangle of harness and sudden hoofbeats. Ross looked over his shoulder and saw a horseman riding swiftly toward them. It was Bruton.

"Get away, boy, lest ye want to be locked in an English prison with the rest of these," the guard called out harshly.

Kettie jumped up and darted away, running toward the cliff. Tam raced after her, barking wildly. Behind them galloped Bruton on his horse. As the steed gained ground, Tam turned and lunged at the horse. Bruton drew his sword, raising it to strike.

Ross, stumbling behind, felt as if he were living a nightmare. In one fleet instant he saw Kettie throw herself between Tam and the sword. The next, he saw a flash of metal and a jumble of hoofs. Then Kettie tumbled over the brink of the precipice and disappeared from sight with a piercing scream.

Ross ran to the spot from which she had fallen. There,

on the rocks below, was her body, just at the water's edge.

One minute she lay limp and lifeless as a rag doll. The next, a giant comber foamed over the rocks, completely covering her body. When the wave at length receded, the ledge where she had lain shone wet and glistening like the rest of the deserted shoreline—and as empty.

Ross lay prone at the cliff's edge, straining to catch sight of a white hand in the water, or a strand of pale hair. He knew full well that Kettie must be dead. She could not possibly have survived the fall to the bottom of the cliff. No one could.

Why not throw himself over the edge after Kettie? There was nothing ahead for him but imprisonment in some English stronghold. He'd rather die quickly and cleanly as Kettie had than rot away inch by inch.

A rough tongue rasped his cheek. Blind fury rose in Ross. If Tam had not snapped at the horse, Kettie might still be alive. He struck at the dog with his fist, and said fiercely, "Begone!"

He hardly saw the animal's startled hurt, but let his head fall forward onto his arms.

Minutes later he heard returning hoofbeats and Bruton's truculent tones. "How could I know the boy would try to save the dog? If ever I see that cur again—" There was no mistaking his lethal intent.

Even after the hoofbeats receded into the distance, Ross lay unmoving. Twilight had thickened when a strong hand shook him by the shoulder.

"Ye'll do nae good here. Come." Duncan Muir's voice was the one stable force in a world gone wrong.

Ross let himself be led back to the center of the field and accepted a handful of oats, all that the ravenous men around him had left of the sackful Kettie had brought. Ross put the oats in his mouth but scarcely tasted them. As in a dream he watched Lachlan stuff the bagpipes into the empty sack.

On every side the captive Scots muttered invectives against the English. On the roadway the guards paced between campfires. The fragrance of roasting mutton wafted cruelly through the night air.

Ross was as unaware of sights and sounds and odors as if he were a thousand leagues distant. In his mind's eye swirled Kettie's white face as it was when she had stood on the ramparts at Tantallon. Her low voice sounded in his ears. "I know what my death will be. I saw myself in a dream, falling down a steep cliff onto rocks, and the sea carried awa' my body. The cliff was like that at the seaward side o' the castle."

The precipice here was so similar to Tantallon's steep cliffs as to have been hewn from the same pattern. Ross was completely unnerved and could not help telling Duncan and Lachlan about Kettie's premonition of her death.

Duncan sighed gently, saying, "Puir wee lass."

But Lachlan shook his head and intoned, " 'Therefore hearken not ye to your prophets, nor to your diviners, nor to your dreamers.' "

Ross turned away in disgust, sorry that he had spoken. Did Lachlan always have to spout Scripture?

Utter exhaustion finally brought sleep. As he sank into oblivion, Ross remembered Kettie's other dreams. She had surely been right when she had envisioned him in the midst of battle. Might her foreknowledge of other things be true? It was very unlikely that so strong a fortress as Tantallon Castle would be breached. It was also highly improbable that he, Ross McCrae, bound for imprisonment in England, would ever sail away across the ocean.

The Moor

In the early morning a thick mist hung over land and sea. The wide vista of the night before was obscured by a wet, gray curtain. When Ross first awoke he thought for a moment that he had been hunting and had spent the night in a Kindonal glen, wrapped in his plaid. Then sick realization flooded over him.

He got stiffly to his feet, fighting the dizziness that swept over him with each movement. The bagpipes lay on the ground in Kettie's sack. It took all his will power to bend down and pick them up and tuck them into the back of his plaid. Kettie had lost her life bringing the pipes to him. The least he could do was keep them safe.

Around him men were rising, shivering with cold and damp, shaking out their sodden plaids. Droplets covered their hair and beards.

Duncan stood awkwardly nearby, cradling his wounded arm. Ross looked at the rough bandage, stiff with hardened blood, and his stomach turned over. Then he realized that

106

no fresh blood was seeping through the grimy folds. That much was good.

The order came to march, and the Scots slogged into line and dragged slowly along the Great Road. Duncan tried to strike up a conversation with the two men just behind.

"What part of Scotland might ye be from?" he asked.

"Just ahead of here, close to the Border," said one. He was thin and wiry, and had a heavy dark beard and beetling brows. "MacKie's my name."

His companion made no reply. He kept his eyes on the road and his lips pressed together.

"Know ye the country well?" asked Duncan of MacKie.

"Well enough." The eyes under the heavy brows bored into Duncan's. "A pedlar gets to know all the tracks and paths."

"A brave lot, pedlars," said Duncan admiringly. "Courage it takes to roam the country as they do."

Ross gave Duncan a sidewise glance. What was he up to? Only last week Duncan had cursed roundly at a pedlar who had sold him a buckle that bent at the first pressure.

By mid-morning the sky had lightened. At the noontime halt a guard tossed filled sacks to the prisoners. Ross ripped one open and plunged a fist inside. A second later he drew out a handful and spat in disgust.

"Horse fodder!" he cried.

"I'm not above eating anything my stomach will take," said Duncan. He picked through the chaff and found a few grains, put them in his mouth, and chewed. Ross did the same, noting that Duncan's usually ruddy cheeks seemed redder than ever, and that his eyes were very bright. The wound in his arm must have brought on a fever.

That night they stopped near the moors. The English formed a ring around the prisoners and set up their tents at intervals. They must have divided the total body of captives into two or more groups, thought Ross. There were certainly not ten thousand men here.

With no shelter and no rations, the Scots bedded down in the rough grass between the Great Road and the sea. As empty of hope as of food, Ross wrapped himself in his plaid and sank down. The worn lengths were poor protection against the piercing wind and night damp. He twisted and turned in an effort to ease his aching body. The days were bad enough, with the agony of having to keep moving. The nights were far worse. Into his tormented brain flashed scenes from the days just past—the shock of the stampeding cavalry's rush, his father's distorted corpse, and over and over again, Kettie's frail form hurtling downward to the sea. When he slept it was no better. He awakened time and again in a drenching sweat of terror. If only Tam were here, he thought. But it was better that the dog be safe and out of reach of Bruton's wrath.

Ross had dozed off sometime during the night when he heard Duncan's voice in his ear.

"Up, lad," came the whisper.

Instantly Ross was wide-awake. By straining his eyes he could make out Duncan's shadowy bulk, Lachlan's stocky figure, and the silhouette of the bearded pedlar.

"The guard's asleep," said Duncan in a barely audible tone. "Can we but steal past him, MacKie can lead us across the moor and into the Lammermuir Hills."

Silently the four crept through the field, past slumbering captives, toward the guard by the roadside. He sat with his hand resting on his musket. Was he indeed asleep? Hardly daring to breathe, they had started to creep past him when his head jerked up.

The Scots froze. Ross's every nerve tautened. Surely the guard could see them and at any moment would cry out the alarm!

Suddenly a tremendous sneeze exploded from the soldier's tipped-back head. He wiped his face with the back of his hand and leaned forward once more to rest his forehead against the musket.

With infinite caution the four prisoners tiptoed onto the road. A few steps more, and they pushed through the low hedge on the other side. Then they stood on the edge of the moor, breathless and still stiff with fear and caution.

When they had gone several rods into the murky darkness, the Scots dared to stand upright and walk. But even then they could not hurry. Traversing a moor was difficult enough in daylight, when one could see the tufted hummocks of grass that provided safe footing. Trying to cross the boggy ground by night was a feat only the desperate would attempt.

Slipping and sliding, Ross followed the dark shape ahead. MacKie was wiry and light of foot, and covered the ground so rapidly that Ross was hard pressed to keep up. Behind him Duncan gave an occasional grunt as he missed his footing. Lachlan brought up the rear.

The pain in Ross's head seemed a part of him, it had been there so long. And now there was a ringing in his ears. But wait. Was it really in his ears? He stopped and listened intently. There it was again, an eerie, plaintive wail coming thinly through the darkness. The hairs on the back of his neck bristled. The moors were supposed to be haunted by the spirits of those who had died on their desolate stretches.

The high notes were louder now. Lachlan must have noticed them, too, for he halted and asked, "Do ye hear anything?"

Again came the sound, and now it was unmistakably a song.

> He's ta'en three locks o' her yellow hair,
> Binnorie, O Binnorie,
> And wi' them strung his harp sae fair
> By the bonny mill-dams of Binnorie.

For an instant Ross fancied that he was sitting in the warm sunlight on the way from Tantallon to the Broxburn,

listening to Kettie's high sweet voice. He could almost taste
the strawberries on his lips.

> *The first tune he did play and sing,*
> *Binnorie, O Binnorie,*
> *Was "Farewell to my father the king"*
> *By the bonny mill-dams of Binnorie.*

In a trance Ross listened. Had Kettie come back to haunt
him? In life she had been anything but fearsome. And she
had denied being a witch.

> *The nexten tune that he played syne,*
> *Binnorie, O Binnorie,*
> *Was "Farewell to my mother the queen"*
> *By the bonny mill-dams of Binnorie.*

The wind lifted the notes. Surely there was more than
one singer—two or even three. Witches were known to go
in threes. Ross's stomach was a hard knot, and his legs
shook with more than fatigue.

Suddenly Duncan gave a shout. "Ho! Who's there?"

The singing ceased. There only the wind's bleak
soughing. Then a girl's voice called timorously, "Can ye
help us? Our ponies are fast mired. We've been singin' to
keep them awake lest they lie down in the mud and go
under."

Ross let his breath out in a rush, almost laughing in relief. At the same moment, loss stabbed him. Kettie, even as ghost or witch, had stirred his heart.

"Keep on wi' yer song," called Duncan. "We canna see ye, but we'll find ye by yer voices."

MacKie muttered, "Why should we lose time and risk getting caught by helping feckless maids?"

"We canna leave them here," said Duncan shortly.

In a few minutes they had reached the girls. There were three, each one holding fast to the bridle of her mount. One pony had sunk belly-deep in the mud.

Feeling for the hummocks, which offered shaky footing, Ross came up beside one of the animals. It gave a snort of fear. He laid a gentling hand on its flank, waiting for Lachlan to find a place to stand. The weaver was searching for a bit of solid ground.

" 'Deliver me out of the mire and let me not sink,' " he said in the special voice he used for Scripture. " 'Let me be delivered from them that hate me.' "

"Are ye ready?" asked Ross, aware of a certain grudging admiration for Lachlan's ability to find a Biblical quotation for any situation.

The two heaved and pulled at the pony's body, straining and slipping. At last the beast struggled free and followed its mistress to firmer ground. Then Ross and Lachlan helped the others. After a few minutes' work all three ponies were safely out of the morass and headed up a slope to drier ground.

"What are three lasses doing on the moor in the nicht?" Ross asked. "Hae ye no fear?"

" 'Twas fear of the English soldiers made us venture onto the moor," said one, her voice shaking.

"We were coming up from Berwick, where we'd been working in the bakery," said another. "The owner got a message yesterday that bread and bakers were needed in Dunbar, and told us to go there. We set off at sundown with all that day's loaves—"

"Loaves of *bread?*" demanded Ross. He had felt no burdens on the ponies' backs.

"We left the sacks back where the ponies were mired. The bread was muddy and not fit to eat."

What was a little mud? Ross scrabbled back to the bog, MacKie beside him. They located two sacks and bore them triumphantly to the others. For a few minutes there was no talk, only the sound of loaves being torn and chewed with ravenous haste.

"Dinna eat o'er much," warned Duncan. "Gie yer stomachs a chance to get used to being aught but empty."

A few minutes later Ross asked the girls, "How will ye get from here to Dunbar?"

"The Great Road loops around the eastern border o' the moor in a half circle. We had thocht to cut directly across the moor and come out on the road farther north, where we'd no' meet the soldiers."

"There'll be soldiers aplenty in Dunbar," said Duncan. "Are ye no' afeard o' them?"

"No' in the town. The crier said there was a paper signed by Cromwell himself, promising his men wouldna harm folk so long as they stayed peaceful."

"We've tarried here o'er long," MacKie said impatiently. "Now we maun be on our way."

"How ye can tell where ye're goin' is beyond me," said one of the girls. "We mean to stay here till it be light. We dare not chance our ponies gettin' mired again."

"I ken the way," MacKie said brusquely. "We need but go west frae the road to reach the hills." He started off with apparent confidence.

"We canna thank ye enough, and we pray that ye get awa' safe," another girl said.

No fool she, mused Ross. She had not needed to ask why four Scots were tramping across the moor at night.

For what seemed a long time they stumbled through the darkness. A full stomach made a world of difference. Ross's legs seemed stronger and his head less painful.

MacKie halted. "The road should be over there." He pointed to the right. "If we go straight ahead, we shall come out in the hills where we'll be safe."

"Are ye sure, man?" Duncan asked. "I would hae said we should go farther west still."

MacKie snorted angrily. "I was raised just t'ither side o' this moor," he said.

Long ago Ross had lost all sense of direction. Now he noted that the wind had dropped, the sky was lightening, and a thick mist hung about them, obscuring all but the nearest objects. He followed MacKie over the rough ground.

They had gone about half a mile farther when a sudden breeze abruptly lifted the mist that covered them. Stark and unprotected they stood in the middle of a bare field which contained not a bush or shrub to hide under.

The wind bore away further curtains of mist. In the next agonizing moment Ross saw a body of milling prisoners directly ahead beside the highway. He and Duncan and Lachlan and MacKie had escaped from one captive group only to blunder directly upon another, farther north on the Great Road.

Without warning a body of horsemen suddenly appeared. Two of them rode apart from the group and urged their mounts outside the hedgerows that lined the road, ready to strike down any captives that might have hidden there. In a minute they would draw near.

MacKie turned. "Run for it!" he shouted, and set out back across the empty moor.

For a second Duncan stood still. Then in a taut voice he said to Ross and Lachlan, "Our only chance is to join the ither captives. Haste ye, ere the guards look this way."

Bending low, he scuttled toward the milling men. Sick at heart, Ross followed, Lachlan close at his heels. The mass of prisoners opened to receive them. They had made their way well into the ranks when they heard a shout from a guard, and turned to look back.

On the barren hillside they could clearly see the stumbling MacKie. Behind him raced a horseman. In a few seconds he had caught up with the fugitive. A swift blow of the saber, and MacKie tumbled to the ground. The guard returned, wiping his blade. "One less to watch over," he said with satisfaction.

Across
the Border

"What's that in yer sack?" a rough voice queried.

Ross jolted to attention. "Bread," he said to the prisoner beside him. "Will ye hae some?"

Almost before he spoke, the bag was torn from his hand. As its contents were dumped on the ground the Scots fell upon them with wolfish cries. Ross managed to snatch one grimy loaf and hide it in his shirt. It should keep him and Duncan and Lachlan going for a few more miles.

A short time later another man asked, "How came ye here?"

Duncan was explaining when Ross felt a thump on his shoulder. He turned, and gave a glad cry. "Hugh MacPherson and Dougal MacFarlane!"

"Aye, and John Davison, too." The slight schoolmaster stepped forward.

For a few minutes they related their experiences, Hugh and Dougal had found each other the day before in the throng of prisoners. They had encountered John Davison the previous night.

"Hae they fed ye well?" asked Duncan grimly.

"A bit o' horse feed yesternoon," said Hugh bitterly.

"Aye, we had the same," said Ross. Cautiously he felt for the loaf. Under the cover of his plaid he drew it out, broke it into three parts, and gave them to Hugh, Dougal, and John Davison. They asked no questions, but stuffed the muddy dough into their mouths, chewing like starved beasts. Ross tightened his belt a notch. He and Duncan and Lachlan would have to do without.

The guards came riding up, ordering the prisoners into line. Hugh and Ross stood side by side. Ahead of them were Duncan and John Davison, Dougal and Lachlan. Just behind walked a stout trader and a sturdy smith from Dunbar.

As they dragged along the road, Ross felt more dead than alive. Most of his strength had been drained by the effort of the night flight. Its futile ending had sapped his spirits.

Hugh must have read his thoughts. "A bitter blow, to come out o' the moor where ye did."

"Aye." Ross could say no more.

"Think ye there'll be another chance to flee?" Hugh's tone was desperate, and his narrow face shone with the determination of a fanatic. "I canna face life wi'out Jeannie and the bairn. I maun get back to them."

"Ye saw what happened back there." Ross jerked his thumb over his shoulder toward MacKie's body.

"Aye. But I maun try." Hugh's eyes had a steely glint.

An hour later the prisoners drew near a stone dovecot
with circular walls that rose to a conical roof. A thick
hedge grew between it and the road. Through its many
small openings a few random pigeons flew.

Ross had been looking off into the distance toward the
sea. When he turned to say a word to Hugh, he saw that
his friend had vanished. A step or two behind him the
branches of the hedge quivered.

Two guards were standing beside their mounts a few rods
to the rear inspecting the animals' hoofs. One man drew
something out from his horse's shoe and both remounted.
Hugh must have taken advantage of their inattention to
slip through the bushes.

As the guards approached Ross, a cloud of pigeons, their
wings beating and whirring, shot out of the dovecot.

"What might cause that?" asked one soldier.

"Likely a weasel hae got into the doocot," said Duncan
in a loud voice.

"More likely a two-legged weasel!" cried the other guard.
Dismounting, he drew his sword, pushed through the hedge,
and disappeared around the dovecot. A few minutes later
Hugh emerged, his hands above his head. The guard gave
him a blow with the flat of his sword.

"Back in line, there," he said gruffly.

Ross let out a breath of relief. Thank heaven that Bruton
had not been there to discover Hugh. Bruton would doubtless have used the sharp edge of his blade.

At mid-morning the dreary column reached the Bounds

of Berwick at Lamberton Toll, where a company of Ironsides and gunners at the alert showed Ross only too clearly
that he was now at the Border march and so passing out of
Scotland. Three miles on, the prisoners reached the walls
of Berwick-upon-Tweed and wearily tramped through the
Scots Gate, where down the years many bloody skirmishes
had been fought to gain possession of the coveted bastion
of a burgh. As they passed through the narrow streets not
a soul was to be seen. Every lane and byway was empty;
no face showed in any window.

Dropping down toward the river, the Scots soon came
within sight of the stone bridge, its fifteen arches proudly
spanning the Tweed's flow. Ross had walked but a few
paces beyond the soldiers guarding the Bridge Gate when
the order came to halt. The prisoners ahead were slow in
negotiating the openings in the two palisades placed near
the bridge's center to provide additional security. With
Hugh on one side and Duncan on the other, he leaned
wearily on the parapet and looked down at the rushing
water. The swirling currents had a mesmeric effect. It would
be an easy matter to leap over and let himself be sucked
down into the dark depths.

As Ross gazed into the water, a sleek wet head broke the
surface, and two round brown eyes looked up into his own.
Ross stared at them in a daze. Could it be true that seals
were human beings under enchantment, as he had been told
when a child? He could hear his old nurse's voice telling
how the seals came ashore on a summer's night, shed their

skins, and danced and frolicked as men and women. There
was a tale of a young fisherman who hid the skin of a
beautiful seal maiden. When the others returned to their
homes beneath the water, she could not find her fur covering and so was forced to stay on land and marry the fisherman. Later one of their children found the skin and brought
it to her. With a wild cry she put it on, ran to the shore,
and vanished under the waves.

Hugh must have heard the same story, for he said
dreamily, "I wonder now, could that be the seal maiden?"

The animal kept its unblinking eyes fixed on the Scots,
its nose wrinkling, and its long whiskers quivering.

Duncan gave a snort of derision. "A fine wife she'd make
—with that mustache!"

Hugh chuckled, and Ross found himself laughing. He
had thought he would never smile again, but here he was,
actually shaking with mirth. Dougal and John Davison, too,
and even Lachlan, were grinning broadly. The seal, as if
embarrassed, sank out of sight.

'Tis strange, thought Ross, that such a little thing could
make us laugh. Ordinarily Duncan's remark would have
brought forth no more than a smile. But the past few days
had been so filled with cruelty and death that their wearied
spirits had responded to even this slight sally.

After a short while the line started moving over the
bridge toward the southern bank and the village of Tweedmouth. As he crossed over the central span of the bridge,
Ross was assailed by a wave of anguish. Here, he felt, he

was really leaving Scotland behind. When, if ever, would he return to his native land? With each footstep an inner voice intoned, Farewell to Scotland. Farewell for aye. His companions, too, were silent. Ross could imagine their thoughts. To his astonishment he saw a tear rolling down Duncan's cheek, cutting a narrow track in the dirt and grime.

At the end of the bridge there was another wait. Then a line of wagons approached, their wheels rattling. Every few feet the vehicles stopped, and guards took sacks from the load and drew near to the captives.

"Food!" exclaimed Dougal.

Ross's mouth was watering at the prospect. He was so hungry that the muddy bread of the night before might never have existed. To each prisoner the soldiers gave three hard biscuits and a measure of peas. Ross held open the mouth of his sporran while the guard poured the wrinkled pellets into the leathern bag. He started to gnaw on one of the biscuits immediately. They were the kind that were used on ships, and baked as hard as boards. He managed to bite off a small piece, and after determined chewing, softened it so that it could be swallowed. Next he tried a handful of peas. They were as hard and dry as the hardtack, but in his half-starved state, utterly delicious.

"Eat easy, men," cautioned Duncan. "Hae pity on yer empty guts. God knows how long before we get more rations."

"I care only for today," said the Dunbar trader. He swallowed peas in ravenous haste.

Now the men were plagued by thirst. Up and down the column came cries of "Water! Water!" Soon the prisoners were led in small groups down a slippery bank to the river's edge and allowed to scoop up water in their hands.

Ross felt so parched that he began to think his turn would never come. When at last he scrambled down the muddy path, he saw a dead cat floating past, its body bloated and legs distended. Revulsion swept over him. Then a guard dealt him a blow upon the shoulder and he tumbled forward, landing with his head and arms in the shallow water. His thirst overcame all squeamishness, and he drank deeply. Surprisingly enough, the cool water cleared his head. When he arose, he felt almost like a human being. But when the guard waved his pikestaff, Ross again knew himself to be a trapped animal.

While he drank, Duncan soaked the caked bandage on his arm. As they waited for the rest of the captives to go down to the river he asked Ross, "Would ye help me unwind this rag? 'Twill shrink tight if I leave it on."

Cautiously Ross pulled away the sodden folds, gradually revealing Duncan's arm, the skin strangely white except where the sword blade had slashed. Ross bit his lips, his stomach churning. The wound looked like raw beef. Blood oozed where the bandage had stuck.

Duncan regarded it jubilantly. " 'Tis not festered," he said. "And look, I can use it still." He moved his arm, then groaned in pain. " 'Twill take some mending yet," he conceded. "I'll let the sun at it whilst the rag dries."

During the afternoon the two bodies of captives were merged into one. Ross saw Bruton ride past on his dun horse, sourly appraising his charges. Murderous hate rose up in him.

That night the Scots lay in a field beyond Tweedmouth. A thin rain fell. Ross huddled, wet and miserable, in his plaid. The man from Dunbar rolled in pain, doubled over with stomach cramps.

" 'Tis the peas," he gasped. "Damned English windy porridge."

Had the man not swallowed the peas half-chewed, he might not be so miserable. Ross was thankful for Duncan's warning. He had eaten only sparingly and had still a good supply in his sporran. But even that fact was eclipsed by his despair.

Now that the Scots were in English territory, would he be able to escape? With every day that they were taken further into England, the chances of getting safely back to Scotland grew less. Tonight the guard had been doubled; there was no hope of flight.

Ross was just drifting off to sleep when something cold and wet pressed against his hand. The next minute a warm tongue lapped his cheek. Ross lifted his arms and drew Tam close. He could feel the dog's heart beating next to his own, and was thankful for the darkness, for he was weeping uncontrollably. Somehow Tam had managed to follow him. What canine magic he had used Ross could only guess.

Sometime before dawn Ross woke in panic. He must send

Tam away before the guards discovered his presence. Rousing the dog, Ross buried his face in the rough fur for a moment, then put his mouth close to Tam's ear.

"Ye maun go," he said in an urgent whisper, "but come back i' the night, for I need ye sair." Then he gave the command, "Begone!" and the collie crept noiselessly away.

Alnwick Castle

One wretched day merged into another. Hours of trudging along the road were followed by interminable waits without shelter, without water, and without food except for what remained to each man of the peas and biscuit doled out at Berwick. That must be guarded too. Starving men were not above stealing from their comrades.

Each morning a few prisoners failed to rise. If a kick from a soldier's boot failed to rouse them, the thrust of a bayonet made certain that the captives were indeed dead. Those still alive were prodded to their feet and forced to march. Many later fell in the ditches, where the guards completed with cold steel what starvation had begun.

Ross lost all sense of time. The only thing he looked forward to was Tam's stealthy arrival through the darkness each night. Even that pleasure was tinged with fear lest Bruton discover the dog's presence. Tam's body grew leaner and his coat was tangled with burrs, but he was faithful in searching out Ross wherever he lay.

A few days after leaving Berwick, the Scots reached the top of a rise and looked down upon a valley through which ran a quiet stream. On the hillside opposite stood an imposing castle, its walls and battlements gleaming in the late afternoon sunlight.

"Yon's the Aln River and Alnwick Castle, the seat of the Percy's," said Duncan. "I came this way with Leven's forces in '44. We Scots had the upper hand then, and occupied Alnwick."

Ross looked down across the lush meadows and calm river to peaceful fields rising toward the castle's broad expanse. So this was one of the fortresses of the Duke of Northumberland. Any other time he would have found it a handsome edifice. Now he could see it only as an enemy stronghold.

Phrases of the old ballad, "The Battle of Otterbourne," ran through his mind.

> *To the New Castle when they came,*
> *The Scots they cried on hight,*
> *Sir Harry Percy, an' thou beest within,*
> *Come to the field and fight.*

Almost without thinking he whistled a few bars of the tune. Hugh caught up the melody, and began singing the words. He had not much of a voice, but he had a good memory, and his tone was clear. Soon others joined in.

> *Sir Harry Percy came to the walls,*

The Scottish host for to see,
And thou hast burnt Northumberland,
Full sore it rueth me.

Suddenly Ross noticed that the captives' gait had changed from an uneven stumble to a measured pace. Heads that had hung low were lifted. Shoulders that had been hunched were thrown back as the men sang verse after verse of the old ballad.

The clip-clop of hoofs rang on the road, and Bruton rode alongside. "Enough of that bawling!" he ordered. "You're to go peaceable and quiet. Do you hear?"

The singing ceased, and the men fell back into their former uncertain shamble. Ross clenched his fists in fury. Could the Scots have not even the pleasure of a simple song?

They crossed the Aln and neared Alnwick Castle. Its walls loomed dark and massive. Above the main gateway, flanked by two square towers, was a stone carving of a shield with a lion rampant and a motto: *Esperance ma Comforte*. Ross noted it wryly. *It could serve us Scots, too,* he thought. *Hope is our only comfort now, and some of us have given up even that.*

Under the great arch of the barbican the Scots passed, and over the drawbridge. Overhead the iron teeth of the portcullis hung in jagged threat. Guards shot hostile glances at the Scots. Now and again one spat toward the ragged captives.

From between huge wooden doors studded with iron bolts, the prisoners emerged into a broad courtyard. Ross looked up at the high curtain walls connecting the corner towers. Could anyone ever escape from this fortress? Around the perimeter of the outer bailey were stables, with horses tethered in long rows just outside the doors. The paving stones were slippery with refuse and offal.

Ahead rose a vast bulk of stone, the inner fastness of the castle. The prisoners were marched to a gateway built into a stretch of masonry on the right. Ross noticed the barred windows of the building just to the left of the entrance.

Hugh must have taken note of them too. "I canna bear it be we put in a dungeon," he said. Something in his strained tone caused Ross to peer at him sharply. Hugh's eyes had taken on a strange gleam. Ross had seen that same frenzied look on a fox penned in a cage outside an Edinburgh tavern.

The next minute they passed through the gateway into a second courtyard, the middle bailey. At the sight ahead Ross felt a new wave of despair. The courtyard was half filled with row upon row of prisoners. Some wore the hodden gray and shepherd's checks of Lowlanders, some the regimental uniform of the regular army, and some the reds, blues, and greens of Highland tartans. A few leaned against the walls, others sat hunched in misery, but the majority lay like limp bundles of rags on the wet stones.

Could these sorry creatures be the gallant soldiers of the

Scottish army, those who had marched out from Edinburgh with such confidence in victory?

As the newcomers merged with the earlier arrivals, Ross realized with a shock that he and Hugh, Duncan and John Davison, even Dougal and Lachlan, were one with these scarecrows. A stranger could not have told them apart. All wore filthy, stained garments, all were unwashed and unshaven, and all drooped with fatigue and near starvation.

Ross found a place near the wall and sank down. Dougal sat near, his knees drawn up and his arms folded around his legs. His once red face was pasty, his formerly round cheeks sunken.

"When do ye think they'll gie us food?" he asked. "I'm that empty me belly's fair forgot what it is to be filled."

Ross swallowed. The night before he had eaten the last of his peas. A few leaves of sorrel stripped from a roadside plant had been his only meal today. "It maun be soon are we to survive," he said.

Far beyond the pain of stomach cramps, he was experiencing other effects of deprivation. His head swam, his eyes ached, and he had difficulty focusing on objects. There was a constant ringing in his ears, and he found it hard to breathe. Moreover, his entire body felt as if it were one vast ache.

Hugh stretched out at Ross's side, his face turned up to the sky. Ross saw how tautly the transparent skin was stretched across his cheekbones.

"I wonder is the sun shinin' in Kindonal this day? Perhaps Jeannie has ta'en the bairn's cradle outside the door whilst she spins. She loves the sun, does Jeannie."

The trader from Dunbar sniffed. "Small good it'll do ye to talk about yer wife. She'll be a widow soon and smilin' at anither."

Hugh scrambled to his feet and drove his fist into the man's face. "Can ye no' let a man dream a bit?"

The Dunbar man made no resistance. He buckled and fell in an awkward heap. "I said but the truth," he mumbled.

"Aye, and that's what hurts," Hugh said, "tho' my Jeannie would ne'er hae eyes for anither."

Ross could almost see Jeannie with her shy smile, her light hair in ringlets about her face, and her eyes as blue as the loch. She had loved Hugh since she was a wee lass, and would never cease caring for him. Of that Ross was certain.

If only he had someone to dream of during these endless tortured days and nights. But there was no girl in Kindonal whom he could love. To those of gentle birth he had dared show no more than courtesy. They and their guardians knew him for no purposeful suitor since for all his closeness to the Laird he held no proper title to any lands. The village lasses interested him not one whit. Their talk was all of weaving and lambings, and their laughter too shrill. Poor Kettie's was the only face that swam before his eyes. But deep within himself he knew his feeling for her had been more of pity than love.

Thoughts of Kettie reminded him of Tam. Where was the

collie now? Had he given up hope of finding his master and sought the trail back to Kindonal? Or had he taken up watch outside Alnwick gates, patiently waiting?

They had all been silent for a spell when Hugh said in a low voice, "Think ye there might be a chance to get away?"

Duncan gave a wheeze that might have been intended as a laugh. "Out o' this fortress? Only as a corpse, I'm thinkin'. I know these walls. Naught but a bird could get out."

"Then we must wait until we be moved," said Hugh.

"*If* we be," said Dougal dourly. He grimaced in pain, and asked, "Think ye we may be fed soon?"

But there was no food given out that day. Ross began to wonder how long he could endure without nourishment. One hour merged into another. The men roused and talked, then lapsed into silence. The sun set and darkness engulfed them.

In the morning a score of men were dead. Scots still having some strength were ordered to pick up the bodies and carry them to the gate. Ross was one of the bearers, and was appalled at how heavy even an emaciated corpse could be.

When he returned from helping to load the bodies on a cart, the trader growled, "Three men from Dunbar there be in that lot, good men that did their work well and sat in the kirk on a Sabbath. What odds to them now the cause of King and Covenant?"

"Hush yer blitherin', man," said Duncan. "No mother's son o' us could sit by and let the English cut off King Charles's head!"

132

The words swirled around Ross's ears. How far away seemed the day when he had first heard Duncan speak so, just after a messenger had rushed into Kindonal Castle bearing the traditional burnt cross of wood that was the signal for the clan to rise in arms.

When a few men had demurred at leaving their families and flocks, Duncan had shouted his statement about King Charles. No atrocity that the English had committed had so stirred Scotland as the execution of the king. To set his son on the throne and so avenge the father's death, the levies had gone off with less reluctance than they might have otherwise, in age-old fealty to chief and monarch.

The Dunbar man said in a low voice, as if to himself, "Had I to do it again, I'd flee to the hills."

Ross could almost agree with him. The cause of King and Covenant might be just and worthy, but was not the cost too great? He thought of the Laird, rich with the wisdom of his years, but dying of the ague in a tent on the field. Had he remained in Kindonal he might still live. He recalled his father, robust, hearty, and blustering—the finest piper in all Kindonal. Now his notes were forever stilled. He remembered others of his clan now dead on the battlefield, and all the army of Scotland's most able men. Only a few had survived, and many of those sorely wounded. He sickened at the memory.

Alnwick's Well

The second day dragged by. No food was given out. More men died.

Ross could feel himself losing touch with reality. To keep some semblance of sanity he began studying the castle's structure. In a corner of the middle bailey, where the Scots were confined, rose two lofty octagonal towers, guarding the entrance to the inmost courtyard. Atop each tower stood life-size stone figures of men, armed with weapons. Through the gateway between the towers flowed constant traffic to and from the inner ward, the very heart of the fortress. A row of castle guards stood between the prisoners and the gate, leaving a passageway for castle residents and workers. Ross could see serving men and women hurrying in and out, some bearing baskets on their arms, others carrying fagots or crates of coal on their shoulders.

Hugh kept his eyes on the puffy clouds that scudded overhead. "At least we're no' shut in a dungeon," he said. "We've air enow and the sky above."

A short time later rain fell in a drenching shower. "The open sky's but scant blessing now," commented Dougal as drops coursed down his matted hair onto his shoulders.

The third day passed. Again no food was distributed. Scores of men died.

Lachlan spent much of his time quoting Scripture. Ross marveled that so much of the Bible was given over to laments.

" 'O Lord, how long shall I cry, and Thou wilt not hear!' " said Lachlan. " 'Even cry out unto Thee of violence, and Thou wilt not save! For the wicked doth compass about the righteous.' "

Ross put his head close to Duncan's. " 'Tis my guess that we be done for," he said.

Duncan frowned, and cast a reproving glance at Ross. "Did Robert the Bruce e'er gie in to hardship and pain and hunger? Nay, that he did not. No more should we, lad."

Ross quelled beneath his gaze. His eyes dropped to Duncan's bandaged arm. "Would ye like me to wrap it up fresh?" he asked. "There might be a clean spot left on the rag."

" 'Tis scarce likely," said Duncan in a grim voice. But he held out his arm.

To Ross's amazement the arm was healing well. A thick scab covered the wound, and on either side were narrow strips of new pink skin.

On the fourth day Ross and Hugh found that they were so weak they could hardly stand.

"We maun make an effort," said Hugh, "or we'll no' be able to leave this place."

Ross laughed shakily. Will we live long enough to leave? he wondered.

Supporting each other, the two moved among the prisoners toward the octagonal towers. A stout woman was coming out of the inner court carrying a wooden bucket of garbage.

As she drew abreast of the captives she snarled in an ugly manner, then flung the bucket's contents among the men. "Why should I walk out to the pigpen with it when there are swine aplenty here?"

The soldiers guffawed. The Scots fell on their knees, rooting like so many hogs for the turnip and apple parings, burnt scrapings from a pot of porridge, and some bones.

Ross saw an object flying through the air in his direction. Automatically he caught it and held it tight against his belt, bending nearly double to hide it. He could feel the grease on his fingers, but dared not let any of the half-crazed prisoners see what he held. He watched Hugh scoop up a rotten apple and hissed, "Back to our men."

Near Duncan again, Ross sat down, drew up his knees, and lifted a corner of his plaid over his prize. It was the remains of a leg of mutton, ragged with chunks of fat and gristle. Never had he seen anything so beautiful. Lowering his head, he took a frantic bite of the fat. Chewing, he knew he must have another taste. But he could feel the others pressed close. Summoning all his will, he passed the bone to Duncan.

There was a ripping sound, then Duncan, his jaws working, passed the trophy to Hugh. Dougal, John Davison, and Lachlan, and even the Dunbar man each had a share. After that Ross had another bite, sucked out the marrow, and ground the small soft bones between his teeth. At the last there was nothing left but a few splinters.

Later in the day Ross and Hugh tried to go back toward the gate on the chance the woman might fling more garbage. But others had the same thought, and the prisoners were pressed so closely that Ross could not make his way through.

Night came again.

By the morning of the fifth day a third of the prisoners had died. The stench of death was everywhere. Most of the men lay so motionless that it was difficult to tell the living from the dead.

We can't go on much longer, thought Ross. He moved his shoulders to ease the constant pain that plagued his body, and felt the bagpipes against his back. As if in a dream he drew out the instrument, fitted the chanter in place, and began filling the bag with air. In his weakness he was hard put to force wind from his lungs into the sheepskin, but at length the bag was hard and taut under his elbow. He struggled to his feet.

"And what might ye be about?" growled Duncan.

"Piping—what else?" Ross said. "It was for that I left Kindonal. And pipe I will whilst I've still the breath to blow."

"Ye're daft, man," Hugh said. But there was a gleam of admiration in his eyes.

Ross pressed air from the sheepskin as he fingered the chanter. First came a tentative squeal, then a rising burst of notes, and finally a very torrent of song. He would play his father's favorite march, the wild, fierce medley that was the very lifeblood of the clan.

With the first notes he stepped forward as in parade, marching in time to the music. On either side men moved back to make way for him. Some who had been lying down sat up. Others raised their heads. A little of the dejection went out of their faces.

Ross had swung into the fierce call to the clan when there was a shout behind him and two guards forced their way through the captives. Hugh threw himself on Ross and snatched the pipes away, struggling to hide them.

Then the guards came up, grabbed their arms, and led the two young men toward the gate.

"Dinna take him," said Ross, pointing to Hugh. "He had naught to do with my piping."

"He's holding the pipes now," said the guard, and cuffed Hugh forward. The bagpipes fell to the ground, and the soldier kicked them aside.

At the gatehouse Ross and Hugh were shoved into a small room. The guard raised a trap door in the floor. Below yawned blackness; a fetid smell arose. A dungeon! Ross could feel his palms sweating. He glanced at Hugh and saw his friend's eyes rolling in terror. Hugh would never survive being shut in that dark hole.

Just then a man thrust his head in the door. "Can ye give me two men to draw water?" he asked. "The well boys are both sick."

The guard let the trap door fall. It slammed into place with a sickening thud. Ross could feel his knees buckling. Suppose they had been on the underside of that door when it came down, shutting out all light and air?

"You can have these two," the guard said, shoving Hugh and Ross out of the gatehouse into the inner courtyard. At the right a ladder leaned against the wall. It led to a shelf about six feet above the pavement. Set into a recess were three arches, beneath the center one the well. Crossing the space above it and extending to the two outer archways was a wooden shaft to be turned by means of wheels at each end.

"Get up there," the guard ordered. The two Scots climbed to the shelf. A soldier followed and chained them beside the wheels.

"Now turn them lively," the guard shouted. "There's a deal of water needed."

A bucket, attached to a long rope, was lowered into the well. A distant splash signified the end of its descent. Then Ross and Hugh turned the windlass to raise the dripping vessel. A manservant stood ready to empty the water into a hogshead. When after repeated drawing of the bucket the hogshead was filled, he went off for another.

Ross and Hugh were turning their wheels when a maid-servant stepped out of a nearby doorway. She must have come from the kitchen, Ross thought, judging by the fragrant steam that floated out the door. She carried a basket of blackened fragments.

"See there," Ross said in a loud voice to Hugh, "if it isn't the same woman who tried to hit us with her slops."

The servant looked up and halted.

"A mighty poor shot she is," Hugh said. "She couldna hit the panniers on a pack horse."

The woman picked up one of the charred chunks. "I'll hit you on your saucy mouth," she threatened.

"Try it and see," Ross called.

"That I will," she said. "I'll hit you both." She set down her basket and began pelting them.

Ross let go his grip on the windlass; Hugh did the same. The wheels spun around, the shaft turned, and the rope unwound speedily. But the two young Scots were too busy catching burnt oatcakes to care. The cakes were like charcoal on the outside, and little better within, but they afforded nourishment. Ross had time to put two in his mouth and three inside his shirt before the manservant came back and drove the woman away.

Hugh, too, had secreted some of the cakes. That night when Ross and Hugh were returned to the middle bailey they gave one each to Dougal, Lachlan, John Davison, and Duncan. The Dunbar man needed none. He lay stiff in death.

Under cover of the darkness Duncan handed Ross his bagpipes. "Ye might yet hae a chance to play these," he said.

For two more days the Scots were kept penned inside Alnwick Castle. On the eighth day the gates were opened, and the captives were formed in ranks and counted. Of the five thousand who had entered Alnwick, only half survived. That ragged remnant was issued a biscuit apiece and led southward, deeper into England.

Morpeth

Two days of weary plodding brought the captives to the town of Morpeth. Here were handsome half-timbered houses and a great clock tower in the market square. The townsfolk lined the streets in open hostility. Some jeered, some threw sticks and stones, but none cast anything remotely edible.

Just beyond the center of town the Scots were forced into a large walled garden that ran down to the River Wansbeck. Ross saw that those ahead hurried into the garden's entrance. A few minutes later he discovered the reason. The ground inside was covered with cabbages.

Fresh green cabbage! The sight alone was enough to half craze a man. With the others Ross surged forward and tore one of the green heads from the ground, stuffing the tough outside leaves into his mouth. Hastily he chewed and swallowed, then ripped off another mouthful and ate that too.

"Take heed for yer stomach," Duncan was warning. " 'Tis not able to churn up all this green of a sudden."

Ross recalled the writhings of the Dunbar man and slackened his jaws' rapid pace. He noticed that John Davison was only nibbling at a leaf.

"My middle's that sore," he declared, "I scarce dare eat a morsel."

Davison was one of the very few who partook meagerly. Like a pack of ravening wolves falling upon a slaughtered sheep the other Scots threw themselves upon the cabbages and devoured them. In a short time not one shred of green remained in the garden.

During the night there was the sound of retching and groaning. In all parts of the garden men vomited, or screamed that their bowels had fair dissolved.

Ross had a pain in his stomach such as he had never known before. He was curled in a tight ball, his arms folded over the knot in his middle, when a dark form crept up to him. Never had he been so glad to see Tam! He threw his arms about the dog, hugging him fiercely, and as the collie pressed close, the pain in his stomach subsided. Tam remained until dawn, when Ross sent him off. Silent as a shadow, the dog leaped over the wall, and was gone.

By the morning's light more Scots were found to have died. Ross averted his gaze from their bodies. It had been enough to listen to their cries in the night.

Some men were so weak that they could hardly stand

upright for the daily count. On the road to Newcastle many died by the way.

"Why did the English not butcher us at Dunbar?" Dougal asked morosely.

"Then their people would hae missed seein' what a fine victory Cromwell had," Duncan answered. "Doubtless he's marchin' through Scotland now, putting all to fire and sword."

"Victory! Hah!" John Davison's usually mild voice was bitter. Then in an apparent change of topic he asked, "Did any of ye ever read the writings of a man called Tacitus?"

"I think the Laird had a book by him. Would it be in Latin?" Ross asked.

"Aye, that's the one. He had no great love for Rome's way of conquering peoples. All he could see was the death and destruction. 'They make a desert and they call it peace,' were his words. And that will be the fate of Scotland."

At that moment a man just ahead tumbled into the ditch, gave a fearful gasp, and lay still. A guard came up and rolled the body over with his foot. The eyes were open in an unseeing gaze; the mouth was slack. Silently the guard observed the body, then walked away.

"Ye'd think they'd gie a man a decent burial," Hugh observed in a shaking voice.

"No need," Dougal said. "The ravens will take care o' him."

He was right. Ravens had been following the Scots since they left Dunbar. Ross dared not look back. He had seen too often the hooked beaks ripping into still-warm flesh. Tacitus's words rang in his mind. "They make a desert and they call it peace." Not only was Scotland being ravaged; there were deserts being created in men's souls that would never flower again.

That afternoon the Scots reached Newcastle, passing through high gates built upon part of the old Roman wall. They were locked up in a great stone church. With the others Ross found a small space on the south aisle where Hugh could look out through a medallion window to the distant stars.

That night food was distributed, three biscuits to a man. Ross chewed on his thankfully, but some of the men were too ill to lift bread to their mouths. In the morning one hundred and forty were too sick to march, and remained in the church.

The sky was overcast when the prisoners stepped out into the day. Despite the threat of rain the street was lined with people who shouted, jeered, and pelted the Scots with rotted vegetable marrows and other filth.

"They hae not yet forgot how we trapped them within the city's walls in '44," Duncan said. "Six weeks we kept them penned up here. 'Twas told they ate e'en the rats."

"A rat sounds no' too bad," said Dougal, "be he fat and meaty."

Ross felt his gorge rising.

At the bridge across the Tyne the crowds thinned to a few sullen onlookers. Outside of Newcastle the road was clear save for an occasional farm wagon piled high with produce, or a string of pack horses, their panniers laden with mackerel and sprats from the coast.

Just beyond the thick hawthorne hedge at the roadside flashed a bit of brown fur. A badger or marten, thought Ross. A mile later he caught the quick flirt of a plumed tail. Could Tam still be following? In the afternoon Ross saw a collie racing across a distant hillside. There was no mistaking that familiar silhouette. He began to long for the night and Tam's return.

While twilight thickened the prisoners staggered on. Despite the tortoise-like pace and the occasional fall of a dying man, they had covered the distance from Newcastle to Chester-le-Street in half a day. Soon they must approach Durham. The last roadside sign had said it was three miles distant.

Just as darkness fell, the train of captives crossed over the River Wear into the town of Durham. The line moved through a narrow street to an open market place lit by guttering torches, then turned right and climbed steeply. At the top of the ascent was a large open space, and beyond it the black outlines of a vast Norman church. Ross's eyes moved up the mighty exterior, its lower windows dimly winking with lights. Up and up he gazed to the central tower. By the time he had followed its outlines to the top, his head was bent far back. Never had he seen a tower so lofty.

The Scots were led to the northwest porch. As he approached the massive doors, Ross noted an intricately worked iron knocker in the form of a human face. He would have laughed aloud could he have summoned the strength. A sanctuary knocker! He had heard of such. In times gone by a fugitive could find refuge and safety here by lifting this piece of metal. Had ever fugitives been in more need than he and his fellows? Passing by, Ross reached out and lifted the knocker. It fell with a sharp clang. The appeal was not unanswered. A second later Bruton hit Ross's knuckles with the stock of his musket.

Within, all was dim and cavernous. A few cressets gave but feeble light. Ross had an impression of great circular stone columns rising far up into murky blackness. Carved stone figures on massive tombs lined the aisles.

In one corner lay a heap of straw with which the Scots were ordered to make pallets. This was the first time that bedding of any sort had been provided. Did this mean that their imprisonment here would last longer than a night or two? Ross was too weary to ponder the possibility. He gathered an armful of the dried grass, spread it on the cold stone floor, and was soon asleep. His last thought was of Tam. Was he lurking outside the cathedral? And how long would even his rare fidelity keep him waiting there?

Durham
Cathedral

When daylight filtered down through the cathedral's lofty windows, Ross could examine its cold and drafty interior. The stone walls were fortress-like; each door was barred and guarded. Escape seemed impossible.

A double row of circular columns ran the length of the nave, and were covered with deeply incised carvings, the cuts broad and deep enough to accommodate a man's hand. The design on each was different, spiraling or zigzagging upward in its own special pattern. In vaulted grandeur the nave stretched to the distant apse and altar. Where the transept crossed, the central tower rose to such a height that Ross could see only shadows far above.

At the end of the south transept the wall was nearly covered by a large, elaborately carved wooden clock. Its four brightly painted and gilded dials told not only the minutes and hours but also the months, the days, and the phases of the moon. Despite the fact that it was of English make, Ross could not stifle his admiration. Never had he seen a more beautiful piece of workmanship.

With the other Kindonal men he made his way past the magnificent carved-stone altar screen, the lofty bishop's throne, and the high altar. Behind it was a slab marking the grave of Saint Cuthbert, whose bones had been brought to Durham in 995, over three centuries after his death.

Now and then Ross passed a man retching and gasping in pain. The chill damp seemed to penetrate one's bones, and Ross was shivering as he stopped to look at the elaborate tombs and marble effigies on either side of the main aisle.

"Here lies Ralph Lord Neville, and Lady Alice his wife," John Davison read. He peered at the date. "Was he not the same Neville who led the men of Northumbria to defeat the Scots under King David the Bruce?"

"Aye, he maun be the same," said Duncan. " 'Twas called the battle of Neville's Cross. See, here is anither Neville tomb, that o' Lord John and Lady Matilda. Would ye look at the wee figures carved all around the base?"

"When did the battle take place?" asked Hugh.

"A bit more than three hundred years ago," Davison said.

How many Scots died that day at Neville's Cross? Ross wondered. Or were taken prisoner? Had those Scots of long ago suffered the same agony as the captives of Dunbar?

They had started to move on when three men came up behind them. One kicked at the tomb. Another spat on the marble figures.

"Three hundred years or no, I say may the Nevilles be damned!" he said.

"Aye, a curse on the Sassenachs!" cried his companion.

Ross could feel an answering hatred rising within him.

Later in the day guards brought in great hampers of biscuits and hogsheads of water. One by one the Scots were lined up and given their allowance of bread and a drink of water. As they passed by, a guard counted their number.

Ross heard him say, "There be thirty less than yestreen."

A second soldier commented, "How so? They be fed the same as any prisoners."

" 'Tis not from lack of food they die now. 'Tis a sickness. Have you never heard of the bloody flux?"

The other drew back. His ruddy face had turned white. "Think you it might afflict us?"

"God forbid. Have you heard their moans? As if hot irons were burning out their vitals?"

Ross was shoved along out of earshot and heard no more. He gave a wide berth to the recumbent bodies on the thin straw pallets. The guards were not the only ones who feared this sickness.

The next day twice thirty men died, and the day after, twice that number again. The illness increased among the survivors, and the groans and retching were fearful to hear. The stench of sickness hung heavily upon the cold, damp air.

The following morning a group of English officers

entered the cathedral, escorted by armed guards. Many held handkerchiefs to their faces; they remained only a short while. Soon those Scots most sorely afflicted were carried away.

"To the Bishop's Castle," a guard ordered. Ross remembered an imposing edifice at the farther end of the open green.

At noontime one of the great doors was opened. Eight men entered bearing baskets of coal. Soon fires burned at various spots. Those captives well enough to stand crowded about the flames.

The same eight servants next brought in large iron pots filled with thick, bubbling stew. *Hot food!* Ross could scarcely believe his senses. After the starvation rations of the past weeks, the smell of meat and vegetables was intoxicating.

The next moment he was being shoved and pushed toward the caldrons in a mob of half-crazed men. Only the bared swords of guards stopped the frantic onrush. Then came an almost unbearable delay while the men were made to form the usual line. And at last the stew was ladled out. When all had been distributed, the servants and guards departed. The Scots were left to their own devices.

A wooden bucketful for each six men was the rule. Ross could feel the saliva welling as he and Dougal carried the bucket to a corner. They set it on the floor, and the others gathered around. Even John Davison's eyes gleamed greedily. For a few moments no word was said. Each man thrust his begrimed hand into the mixture, scooped up a portion, and shoved it into his mouth.

Ross hardly stopped to chew. He swallowed rapidly so that he could stuff more into his mouth—and more. There was beef in the stew, and cabbage, and the whole was thickened with oats. Never had food tasted more wonderful. Even the rich smell of it was heartening. He was about to dip his hand in again when he saw Duncan's brawny arm raised threateningly.

"Be ye men or beasts?" he asked. "Ne'er hae I seen a more sluttish band. Do ye keep on in this wise ye'll be pukin' up every bit."

Ross gulped. Was he imagining it, or was his stomach heaving dangerously?

"Perhaps we should bide a bit and let our bellies get used to the shock," John Davison ventured.

"Nay," Dougal cried. "I say we maun eat now whilst the food is hot. Do we wait, they may take it awa'!" He plunged his hand into the bucket, and brought up a dripping fistful.

"Duncan is richt," said Hugh. "We maun bide a wee time an' then 'twill set better."

"Aye, 'twere best no' to be in haste," Lachlan offered, and added piously, " 'The Kingdom of God is not meat and drink.' "

Reluctantly Dougal accepted the decision. He sat staring at the remaining stew with voracious eyes. Duncan held the bucket firmly on his knees. His wounded arm had healed so well that he was once more a person to be reckoned with.

"An hour by yon clock," he announced. "Then we can eat what's left."

As one man the group fixed their eyes on the dial. Ross thought he had never seen hands move so sluggishly. It took an age for them to cover five minutes. Finally the longer hand reached the half hour mark. Then it crept slowly toward the hour.

A short distance down the aisle a man cried out in pain. "Water," he said. "Water." Then he doubled up.

None of the men near him paid any heed. When he called out again, Duncan shoved the bucket into Hugh's hands. "Take this till I can get a swallow for the puir devil."

A few minutes later he waved his arm and called out, "Ho, McCrae, can ye gie me a hand?"

Ross made his way to the sick man. The sight and stench nearly made him turn back. The sufferer lay in a pool of filth. Duncan was bent over him, attempting to give him a drink.

"Will ye fetch some fresh bedding?" Duncan requested.

Thankful to get away, Ross crossed the cathedral and gathered up an armful of straw. After he spread it out, he and Duncan lifted the wasted form onto the pallet.

Duncan looked at the clock. " 'Tis time for the rest of our meal," he said, and led the way back to the Kindonal men.

As they drew nearer, they could see thrashing arms and

legs, and in an instant the empty bucket rolled across the floor, a trail of stew running onto the befouled stones. A man nearby snatched up the container and thrust his head inside, lapping the broth that clung to the sides and bottom. Others attempted to gather up what had fallen on the floor.

Ross could make out Hugh and Lachlan on top of Dougal, hitting him again and again with their fists. John Davison crouched at one side, his usually serene countenance contorted in fury.

"Dougal was that greedy he snatched the pottage from Hugh and began to eat before the hour was quite up. Lachlan tried to get the bucket away from him, but ye can see what befell. And now the food is spent."

Duncan laid a strong hand on the struggling trio. "Cease yer battlin'," he said. "The evil's done, and there's naught to gain but a lesson. If Dougal likes not our ways, let him fend for himself. There be ithers he can join."

Lachlan sat up and pointed an accusing finger at Dougal. " 'They are greedy dogs which can never have enough,' " he intoned.

Dougal lurched to his feet. "I was that starved," he began in a trembling voice. One eye was bruised and swelling. Blood ran from his lip.

Hungry, was he? Wasn't every man of them half out of his mind with near starvation? Ross clenched his fist. For a minute he had all he could do not to bring it down on Dougal's head.

Was a man's own hunger any excuse for making five others do without half their first decent meal in weeks? In another second he'd be throwing Dougal to the ground. Trembling with rage, he walked down the north aisle, past the choir, and in front of the vast altar.

Back along the south aisle he stumbled, hardly knowing where he walked. He passed the sick man on the fresh pallet of rushes but scarcely saw his feeble glance of gratitude. He passed under the great clock, barely noting the hands pointing to October on the dial of months, and to the 31st on the dial of days. As from another world he heard a voice remark, " 'Twill soon be All Hallows Eve. Think ye the spirits will walk here tonight?"

Just ahead beyond the transept a knot of men had gathered around the Neville tombs. Two were carrying a heavy stone bench. The others drew back to let them into the circle. The pair swung the bench; there was a dull thud as stone met stone.

"Ding it again!" chorused the group.

The two swung the heavy bench once more. This time a sharp crack accompanied the thud.

"Och, the head came off, neat as King Charles's!" Brawny hands lifted the marble likeness of Lord John Neville and held it aloft. A second later they dashed it furiously onto the floor.

"Would it were Cromwell's!" cried a voice thick with hatred.

The crowd moved in. One man used the severed head

to hammer at the hands and arms of the effigies. Others repeatedly slammed the bench against the figures. A stone foot broke off, and another head.

Suddenly Ross was filled with consuming rage and the need to avenge the injuries inflicted upon the Scots by the English. Picking up a chunk of stone from the floor, he began to batter at the marble sculptures. A red haze obscured his vision. He had never before known such insensate hatred. Again and again he struck at the effigies, each blow with fierce intent.

One of Neville's countrymen had killed Black Donald. Thus Ross would strike him who had caused his father's death!

An English soldier had brought about Kettie's fatal fall. How Ross would like to rain blows such as these on Bruton!

English guards had starved and killed his fellows. What he wouldn't give to deal them the same treatment!

At length his weakened muscles would no longer obey his will. He reeled back, hands stinging and arms aching from the stone's impact. Another man took his place. Splinters of marble flew through the air. Soon the Neville tombs were battered beyond any possible resemblance to the titled nobles in whose likenesses they had been sculpted. Even the small figures carved on the base received their share of punishment. Each was beheaded with vengeful fury.

All
Hallows Eve

In a daze Ross tottered toward the south transept, and leaned in a corner near the great clock. Something was pressing against his back. He turned and saw that it was the handle of a small door he had not noticed before. Of course it must be locked. The English would have made certain that every exit was closed securely.

Nevertheless he tried the handle and pushed against the panels. To his amazement the door turned on its hinges. Swiftly he slid through the opening and closed the door behind him, his heart pounding at the prospect of escape.

As he moved forward into murky dimness, his foot struck a stone step, and his fingers met the central column of a curving staircase. He started to spiral upward through the shadows. Wherever the steps led, it would be better than the prison he had left.

Soon he came to a slit in the wall, and looking down, saw an inner courtyard with soldiers standing guard. He continued to climb. The stairs went up and up. Just as his head began to swim from the constant turning he reached a place where the direction of the staircase reversed.

At length he came to a landing where wooden planks spanned the space under a low roof. This bridge must pass over the ceiling of the south transept. Crossing over, he found more stairs leading upward, and pursued those. When he thought that he could not climb another step, he saw light ahead and emerged onto a roof.

A strong wind buffeted him, nearly taking his breath away. He clung to a support and looked down. For a moment he gasped in fear. Never before had he experienced such height. Far, far below lay the green forecourt of the cathedral. The Bishop's Castle at its edge looked like a toy and the guards pacing up and down like insects.

He thought of Kettie plunging to her death from a height less than this. Temptation assailed him. How simple to take one step over the edge and end the misery of captivity.

For a long time he crouched near the doorway, looking down from the top of the tower, his hand frozen in its grip on the stonework. One part of his mind registered the layout of Durham. He noted the roads going to the market square, and the two bridges leading out of town, one to the north, the other to the south. Should he ever escape, it would be helpful to know the quickest route out of the city. At the same time, another part of his mind was grappling with the grisly realization that his attempt at escape was a flat failure. The doorway he had entered with such hope had led only to this tower.

At last he took one final breath of the good fresh air, and began the downward trip. Around and around he went, until he came out at the landing and the wooden bridge. As he crossed it, a ray of sunlight shone through a narrow slit in the wall and lighted a black garment hanging near the head of the stair.

Ross reached out and touched the cloth. It was a good wool and would help to keep him warm at night. He lifted it off the nail, shook it out, and saw a hooded cassock such as monks used to wear. Ah, but it was dusty! It must have hung there for years. He rolled it into a tight bundle, stuck it under his plaid, and continued the descent.

Corkscrewing downward, feeling his way from step to step, Ross remembered the coiling stairs of Tantallon Castle. For a minute he could almost feel Kettie's small cold hand in his, and hear her faint voice in his ear. He listened for her words. Surely she had some message for him. The moment passed, but when it had gone, an idea filled his mind that was so fantastic he hardly dared pursue it.

Tonight would be All Hallows Eve, the night when ghosts and spirits walked abroad. Could he not dress in the monk's robe, trick the guards into thinking he was a ghost, and make his way out of the cathedral? The best time would be when the soldiers were about to leave after their evening tally of prisoners. With luck he could slip out while the doors were unlocked.

Where he would go once he was free of the cathedral was the simplest part of the plan. The remembrance of Kettie had been like a signpost in his mind. He would make for the mighty stronghold of Tantallon. He knew the breadth of its walls, the height of its towers, and the abundant store of cannon and arms. He would make for the seacoast, then skirt along the shore, hiding in caves and eating clams and mussels until he reached the castle. The prospect was exhilarating. He fairly floated down the remaining turns of the staircase.

Almost before he knew it, Ross had reached the bottom step, slipped out through the door, and closed it behind him. He hardly noticed the metallic click as he pulled the door shut.

His thoughts in a whirl, Ross made his way back through the cathedral to the Kindonal men. Lachlan was glowering at Dougal; John Davison and Duncan were deep in a discussion of military tactics. "Had I been in command at Dunbar," Davison said, "I would not have ordered our men down from the heights of Doon Hill, not for a hundred ministers of the kirk."

Ross found Hugh studying his bruised knuckles. "To think that I'd turn on one of my friends," Hugh said. "My mind's fair unsettled by all this. Get I not a grip on meself, 'tis a puir husband I'll be to Jeannie, and a worse father to the bairn." He smiled wanly at Ross.

Ross regarded his own fist, lame from his assault on the Neville tombs. "Aye, we're none of us the same," he said shortly. But not for long, he thought. Soon he'd be out in the open, heading for the Border and Tantallon. That he could make his way back to the castle he had not the slightest doubt. It was a pity that he could not take Hugh with him, but the cassock was large enough to cover only one man.

"Who would hae thought that we would come to this?" Hugh mused. "At the first I was sure I would get away. Naught could keep me frae Jeannie, I swore. But now I know 'twas but an idle dream. I'll die here like the rest of these puir wretches."

Why must Hugh talk so sorrowfully during the little time that remained for Ross to be with him? "Ah, dinna take on so," Ross urged. "Ye look well enough to me."

"For how long will I?" Hugh asked. "Till tomorrow? Or maybe a week hence? Nay, we'll all die o' the flux. We canna get awa' from it. I care not for meself. All that grieves me is Jeannie."

A vision flashed into Ross's mind of Jeannie's tearful face as the clan marched away to war. How he had wished then that some girl would weep her heart out for him. But the only girl who had ever cared for him was Kettie, and she was dead.

Yes, Kettie was dead. Again Ross felt the horror of her fatal drop from the cliff. Once more he saw the wave wash over her still form, and the glistening, empty rock where she had lain.

But Jeannie was alive. And so was the bairn that was the fruit of her love and Hugh's. There were two living souls awaiting Hugh's return. Two souls whose lives would be forever bleak should Hugh die. And die he well might, here in this hellish hole.

For a few seconds Ross turned over a new plan in his mind. He'd best act at once. Were he to deliberate he might lose his courage.

"Hark to me, Hugh," he said. "I've an idea whereby ye can escape within the hour. Mind what I say now, for we've little time."

As Ross outlined the scheme, new ideas came to him. He drew Duncan and Davison into the plot. And by the time the guards came in for the evening inspection, the Kindonal men were ready.

In a shadowy side aisle, Ross and Hugh stood waiting. Hugh was wrapped in the cassock, the hood drawn over his head so that his white face shone but dimly within the dark folds.

Ross held the chanter to his lips, his hands shaking as his fingers sought their places. He could feel the sweat slippery on his palms as doubt assailed him. Surely he had been daft to have conceived so daring a plan. Could they hope to succeed in it?

Beside him Hugh was equally distraught. Under his breath he was whispering almost inaudibly the Latin phrase that John Davison had taught him, the blessing used by monks in olden days. He lifted one hand, and made a trembling sign of the cross.

Putting his lips close to Ross's ear, Hugh mumbled, "Of a

sudden the words hae gone frae me thochts altogither. Can ye bring them to mind?"

"*Pax vobiscum,*" Ross was prompting, when he saw that the soldiers had completed their cursory rounds and were heading toward the main doors.

Ross jabbed Hugh with his elbow. "List ye now to Duncan," he hissed.

As the guards passed Duncan, he asked in his booming voice, "Heard ye the sound of music as ye walked aboot? There hae been strange goings on here since dusk."

The guards looked around nervously.

"Would ye no' leave a soldier or two inside, this being All Hallows Eve?" begged John Davison. "I've a vast fear o' witches and spirits, and 'tis said that they are wont to gather here this nicht."

"A pox on you and your notions," the guard said gruffly.

Ross blew into the chanter, and felt a thrill of triumph as an eerie strain of music floated fitfully in the air, and the soldiers clutched at one another.

"Did you hear anything?" one asked the other.

Ross gave Hugh a shove. "Gae alang wi' ye," he breathed into the cowl. That was all he had time to say. The next minute he had put his lips back to the chanter and produced another series of minor notes. As Hugh moved off toward the great doors, Ross stole silently down the aisle to a dark alcove, and again loosed a plaintive snatch of melody. The music rose up into the dusky heights of the cathedral and floated about in a manner far more ghostly than he had anticipated. His scalp was prickling, whether from excitement or the spell he was producing, he could not tell. He only hoped that English scalps were prickling also.

Ross watched Hugh's black-robed figure move out of the shadows of the side aisle. It came into the circle of light near the door just as the two guards were about to make their exit.

"Who goes there?" challenged one.

A sepulchral voice intoned, "*Pax vobiscum.*" The robe seemed to float toward the open doorway.

Ross held his breath. Had Hugh forgotten the rest of his lines?

He saw a pale hand thrust from the cassock to make the sign of the cross. "*Pax vobiscum,*" the hollow tones repeated, "*in nomine patris et filii et spiritus sancti.*"

If he had not known the truth, Ross would have sworn that he was seeing a spirit. The guards must feel the same. One had ducked behind a pillar. The other recoiled and put his arm in front of his face as if to ward off evil. While he stood thus, the cowled shape slipped through the doorway. Where Hugh had stood was empty space.

Ross let out his breath in a long sigh. He saw the first guard come out from behind the pillar and heard him say in a shaky voice, "Should we report to the captain that we saw Saint Cuthbert's ghost?"

For a moment Ross thought he was going to explode in laughter. Saint Cuthbert, indeed! Just in time he clamped

his jaw tightly shut. What had begun as a guffaw ended in
a muffled cough.

"We'd best not. He'd never believe us. Nor would I had
I not seen it." The second soldier rubbed his eyes.

" 'Tis gone now," the first guard affirmed. "We'd best go,
too, ere we meet any more such tonight."

They went out, slamming and locking the door behind
them.

As the metallic clang echoed through the vaulted spaces,
Ross ran down the dark aisles to the Kindonal men. In
jubilation and triumph they clapped one another on the
back.

"A bonny nicht's work," exulted Duncan.

"Aye, it went off better than I'd've thocht," said Davison
in satisfaction.

"Did ye hear the bit about Saint Cuthbert?" asked Ross,
letting out the laughter that had been locked inside him.

"God bless the good saint!" said Lachlan in rebuke.

Ross bit back a retort. He could do without Lachlan's
piety for once. However, all that mattered was that Hugh
had made his escape. He was probably well away from the
cathedral by now, and if he remembered Ross's description
of streets and byways, he should soon be outside Durham. In
the black cassock, with his face hidden by its cowl, he could
hardly be seen. And if he was seen, he could again im-
personate a ghost. Hiding by day and traveling by night,
buoyed up by his love and longing, Hugh might well reach
home and Jeannie.

The
Clock

The morning after Hugh's escape, Ross woke to the acrid smoke of feeble fires, the fetid stench of sickness, and the groans of the dying. He looked at the flattened straw that had served as Hugh's bed and felt a pang of loss.

Since early boyhood Hugh had been his friend. The two had shared many a confidence during their growing years. Ross had discussed his early problems with Hugh and confessed his doubts as to the future. Hugh had responded with a cheerful acceptance of life's disappointments that had made Ross ashamed of his dissatisfaction.

The memory gave Ross heart to thrust aside his loneliness. All that mattered was that Hugh had gotten safely away from the cathedral. He must be well away by now. Had he been captured, he would surely have been brought back to this stony prison.

But underneath Ross's satisfaction over Hugh's escape rankled the knowledge that except for his sudden generous impulse, he might be the one hurrying northward in the open air under the broad sky.

"Hugh would ne'er hae such a sma' thocht," he said to himself. But all through the day he was tormented by visions of Hugh. Now he could see him lying hidden in a thicket, his head pillowed on fragrant leaves. Or he could picture him creeping behind hedgerows, knee-deep in tall grasses and flowers. In a few days' travel Hugh could reach the border and would once more tramp through gorse and heather. For a moment Ross could almost smell the wild scent of the Scottish hills and feel the fresh breath of a highland breeze. Ah, he had been a fool to give up his chance of freedom!

All day Ross fought with himself, each moment hating his imprisonment more and more. Around him sounded the groans and curses of stricken men, punctuated by occasional blows on the Neville tombs. The marble figures had been reduced to ugly, truncated lumps of stone. Remembering their former beauty, Ross eyed them in sick contrition. How could he have taken part in such senseless and futile destruction?

The guards now left the prisoners alone for large periods of time. They had no wish to catch the dread disease. Of Bruton, Ross had not had a glimpse since entering the cathedral. Doubtless he had been sent on to other duty.

Ross's one distraction was studying the ornate clock that took up most of the space on the end wall of the south transept. Prior Castell's clock, the guards called it. The handsomely carved case was painted in glittering gold, rose, and turquoise. Ross never failed to marvel at the intricacy of the gears and wheels that kept track of many measures of time and to admire the cunningness of the mind and fingers that had conceived and fashioned the clock.

Late in the afternoon Ross was gazing at the clock when he saw two prisoners laboriously drag a stone bench to a position under the masterpiece. In a few minutes they drew up another, and after much effort, succeeded in placing it on top of the first. One of the men climbed up and began to wrench at the ornately carved frame.

Ross jumped up and ran toward the men. "What might ye be doin' to the clock?"

"Gettin' some wood for a fire. 'Twill warm us for an hour."

"Take not the clock," urged Ross. "We need it for telling the time."

"Time means naught to us," the man declared. "The clock is English, like the tombs. Ye were quick enow to hammer at those."

For a moment Ross was silent. The Neville effigies had been a symbol of the English army that had brought defeat and humiliation to the Scots. They were appropriate targets of Scottish retribution. The clock was different.

How explain that in this gray prison the clock's gilt and rose and turquoise were tokens of the colors of the world outside? That the movement of the hands was a reminder that somewhere men moved in purposeful activity? That the click of the machinery was proof that the human mind could invent something other than weapons for killing and maiming human beings?

" 'Tis the only civilized thing left to us!" Ross cried. The words echoed through the lofty transept. As he finished speaking, he knew his attempt was hopeless. Unmoved, the man continued to wrench at the carved frame.

"Stop him! Stop him before he tears down the clock!" Ross shouted to the other captives. His words were swallowed up in the cathedral's vast space. The Scots sat or lay in dreary stolidity. How could he pierce their apathy?

Frantically Ross looked about. Duncan was in a corner, holding the head of a sick man.

Ross hurried to him. "They mean to burn the clock!" he cried. "Help me to stop them!"

Duncan looked up. "There's naught I can do. They heed no man's words." He turned back to his patient.

A flicker of an idea came to life in Ross's mind. They might heed no man's words. But there was something to which they must pay attention. The Scot had not been born who could turn a deaf ear to the bagpipes.

Back to his pallet he hastened, and lifted the instrument from its hiding place under the straw. Hurriedly he wiped the blowpipe on his arm, set it to his lips, and began to force air into the sheepskin. He raised angry eyes to the clock and saw that the men had succeeded in tearing off a part of the lower fretwork. He must hurry!

Beneath his arm he could feel the sheepskin swelling. Was there air enough in it now? He forced out a tentative note. It was scarcely audible. He must make a greater effort!

In his inner ear rang his father's voice as he had spoken long ago on the shore of Loch Ruich. " 'Tis no' just the notes ye maun learn. 'Tis the reachin' down deep in yer ain soul to gie ithers the spirit they hae forgot."

Had he any spirit left? Was there anything in his soul to reach for? Pain stabbed at his ribs as he again filled his lungs. Ignoring the ache, he blew fiercely into the blowpipe, and felt the sheepskin grow hard and firm. One mighty rousing note he played, then launched into the music that had been his father's favorite.

First came the grave steady rhythm of the march, filled with motion. Gradually quickening as if in conflict, the notes ran on in noisy turbulence.

Ross could see ailing men lift their heads, others rise to their feet. The two men at the clock had stopped their work of destruction and were peering toward him.

Now came the swelling of the wild notes into flourishes of triumph. Ross put every ounce of effort into sounding the last chords with the victorious might they demanded. As the final echoes died away, the man on the stone bench raised his arms again. In another minute he would begin to wreck the clock itself.

Ross's eye lit on the carving of a flower at the top of the clock. "The thistle!" he shouted at the top of his lungs.

"The flower of Scotland! Would ye let harm come to our nation's blossom?"

There was an answering cry from the men around him. They surged forward toward the clock. "Nay, touch not the thistle!" they cried. Three grasped the legs of the man on the bench and brought him down in an awkward tumble.

"Let the clock and the thistle be!" they ordered. With cuffs and blows they made their demand clear, until the two men left the transept and retreated to a far corner.

Ross pressed the air from his bagpipes, feeling strangely at peace with himself. Gone was his regret over giving up the chance for escape. Instead he wondered if he could rightly have savored freedom, knowing that Hugh could not share it with him.

At least he had accomplished some good these two days past. Hugh had been saved, and the clock as well. Perhaps tomorrow he would find a way to save himself.

A Meeting
and a Parting

The next morning a rotund English officer passed among the Scots, pointed to this one and that, and ordered them to go to the northwest doorway. Ross and Dougal were among the forty thus chosen. When all had gathered, they were issued rough brooms and large baskets.

"Nowhere have I smelt even a stable that stank so foul!" said the officer. "Make it as clean as you can."

Ross began sweeping. He had never thought to be wielding a broom, yet here he was, and thankful for it. Lifting the filthy straw in his hands when he had helped Duncan with the sick had been hardly to his liking.

When all was swept, buckets of water were brought. Ross first washed his face and hands, then swished water over the floor and scrubbed at the worst spots with his broom. It did little good, it seemed to him, merely spread the foul odors still more.

In spite of hot meals and fires, the flux continued to spread. Rations of boiled milk were distributed, but new men sickened each day, and others died. Half the captives must have perished, Ross thought. Mercifully the Kindonal men had been spared.

Then Dougal fell ill. One noontime he stopped eating and said with a puzzled look, "The pottage tastes sour. I like it not."

Ross ran his tongue over his lips. The stew tasted all right to him.

That night Dougal was painfully ill. Lachlan hovered over him, saying, " 'Whom the Lord loveth He chasteneth.' "

Dougal looked up at Ross. "Ye dinna think this sickness is a judgment on me for greediness when we first were given the pottage?"

Ross was torn with pity. "We were all greedy that day," he said shortly. "Ye but lost yer head for a time." And so did many of us, he added silently, with a glance at the mutilated tombs.

Duncan laid a reassuring hand on Dougal's shoulder. "There's anither bit o' Scripture I want ye to think on, lad. 'God is our refuge and strength, a very present help in trouble.' "

Ross looked up in surprise. It was the only time he had ever heard Duncan quote from the Bible.

For a day and night Dougal lay in pain. Ross could hardly bear to hear him groaning or to see him writhing in agony. His end was not easy, and when at last he lay quiet and still, Ross could feel only relief. Beneath it was cold fear. How soon before the other Kindonal men were stricken?

The day that Dougal's body was carried out of the cathedral, the rotund officer returned again. This time he asked that all weavers come forward. A dozen men answered the call.

"Do ye think I should gae?" Lachlan asked of Duncan.

"Ye've naught to lose," Duncan replied.

" 'My days here are swifter than a weaver's shuttle, and are spent without hope!' " Lachlan said unctuously. "I'll gae and hope for something better." He left without a backward glance.

Later in the day Ross heard that the Mayor of Durham desired the weavers to begin a trade of cloth such as was woven in Scotland.

The following morning forty men were taken out of the cathedral. The rumor was that they were to serve in the saltworks at Shields. In the afternoon forty more were taken to work as laborers.

"The English maun be gettin' tired o' haein' us for their guests," Duncan said that night. "I wonder if our turn might not come soon."

It came sooner than they expected. Ross was sweeping the floor the next morning when the officer again entered. He waved a document in his hand and called out in a loud voice, "If there be any Highlanders, let them come forward."

From here and there among the shadowy aisles gaunt men rose, gathering tattered plaids about them. Ross threw his broom at a startled Lowlander and made for his pallet.

He picked up the bagpipes, thrust them under his plaid, then joined Duncan and Davison. In his heart was a prayer. "Oh, let them be sending us back to Scotland."

When one hundred and fifty men had been counted, the door was unbarred and the Highlanders filed out of the cathedral. How bright was the sunshine! How green the grass! Had the sky ever been so blue, or the clouds so snowy? And the clean fresh air—had anything ever been so welcome?

Blinking in the unaccustomed dazzle, Ross looked at his fellows. Hollow-cheeked faces streaked with soot, eyes red-rimmed from smoky fires, bodies so thin that they seemed like skeletons—a sorry lot they were. Yet each man's face held a strange light. To be out in the world once more under the open sky was in itself a boon.

The stocky officer stepped forward and held up a document. "I am informed by Sir Arthur Haselrigge that he has received an order from the Council of War in London to deliver one hundred and fifty Scottish prisoners to Augustine Walker in that city. Such prisoners are to be shipped from Newcastle to London with all possible speed."

With all possible speed! Ross almost laughed aloud in derision. After the dragging and halting of the earlier march and the long cathedral confinement, *now* they were supposed to go with all speed!

Without further ado the Scots were marched down the narrow street to the market place. Few guards accompanied them. The English must be sure we'll not try to escape here in this crowded town, thought Ross, or that we're too weak to make the effort.

At the northeast corner of the market square the prisoners were ordered to halt. A woman appeared in a doorway and beckoned to the soldier nearest the Kindonal men. Her voice was raised in anger, and she seemed to be threatening him. He put his hand over her mouth, shoved her into the doorway, and began talking to her in a placating tone. The others guards were out of sight around a corner.

"Shall we make a break for it now?" Ross mouthed in Duncan's ear.

Duncan shook his head. "Nay, look there." He pointed down the street to a distant body of soldiers marching toward the square. "We'd not get far."

Just then there was a clatter of hoofs from the opposite direction. Ross wheeled around. Seldom had he seen finer steeds or more elegantly attired riders—a gentleman in gleaming satin, and a young woman in a cloak of peacock velvet glinting with gold lace.

"Out for a morning ride," said Davison with biting scorn. "Some folk seem no' to ken that the country is at war."

As the horses drew nearer, Ross noted that the gentleman's fine suit and rich cape were wrinkled and stained and that his graying shoulder-length hair was disheveled. The lady was equally travel-worn. Mud soiled the full sweep of her skirts, and she seemed to droop as she sat on her sidesaddle. No morning ride, this. They had been traveling all the night, he was sure.

How strange that no retinue followed them. A gentleman of quality would not ordinarily travel without a groom and manservant. And no lady would go on a journey unaccompanied by her maid.

All at once Ross understood. The gentleman must be a Cavalier, an enemy of the Parliamentarians, fleeing from Cromwell's forces.

The riders slowed near the Kindonal men. Ross lifted his eyes to the face above the blue cloak and saw that its wearer was a girl, probably younger than he. With her light brown hair and finely chiseled features, she might be pretty. Now her eyes were deeply shadowed and her mouth drawn with fatigue. When she looked back over her shoulder, there was naked fear in her gaze.

In a low tone, scarcely audible above the snorting of the horses and the stamp of their hoofs on the cobbles, the girl asked, "Which way do we go now, Father?"

Ross could see that she was making a brave effort to smile, though her voice was thready with weariness.

"This way, Joanna, across the Elvet Bridge," the man said in a guarded tone. His eyes were sunken and his skin gray. "On the other side lives a man who was my friend. Be he still that, he will give us lodging."

He urged his mount forward, and the girl followed. But not before Ross had seen the look of pity she gave to the line of ragged captives. Then the Englishman and his daughter clattered out of sight around a bend of the narrow street.

The whole episode had taken no more than a minute or two. But that had been long enough for Ross to wish that by some miracle, time might be turned back so that he could appear as he had before the battle of Dunbar, and that he might be presented to this young lady as the Laird's ward. For some unaccountable reason he was filled with a desire to protect the girl named Joanna. Roughly he drew a hand across his forehead as if by so doing he could wipe away the thought of her. Dinna be daft, he told himself. Ye're less than scum to her, just one of a tail of savage captives.

A few minutes later the soldiers marched into the square. The guard emerged from the doorway, red-faced and perspiring. Then the entire body of soldiers and prisoners moved across the square and down a street on the other side. They had gone a few rods when three troopers rode up, halted, and looked about.

The leader was abreast of the Kindonal men. He leaned down from his horse and shouted to the nearest guard, "Did you see two travelers, a man and a woman?"

"Not I," said the guard. "I got here but a second ago."

The prisoner behind Ross started to speak. Ross stamped on his foot and said loudly, "They went o'er that brig, no' five minutes past." He pointed toward the Framwelgate Bridge in exactly the opposite direction from the one which the girl and her father had crossed.

The three set off at a gallop.

The man behind Ross rubbed his sore foot angrily. "Why did ye tell such a lie? When the troopers learn they've been tricked, 'twill be the worse for us."

"What odds?" Ross shrugged his shoulders. "I'd do it again to save any puir souls from capture by the Roundheads."

As the words left his lips, Ross remembered the girl's pale face and fearful eyes, and wondered if he had spoken the full truth. Would he have told such a lie for just any fugitives?

The heavily guarded line of prisoners moved forward, crossed the Wear River by the Framwelgate Bridge, and set off along the North Road toward Newcastle. There was no sign of the three troopers. Evidently they had taken the other fork at the end of the bridge to Neville's Cross. Ross hoped that the girl and her father had reached their friend's house, and that he was still friend enough and courageous enough to take them in, fugitives as they were.

The Scots marched silently. Each one is busy with his own thoughts, mused Ross. And dour, bleak thoughts they must be. His mind fastened on memories of Kindonal. Instead of orderly English fields with neat hedgerows, he saw wild glens, thick with heather and bracken. Instead of gently rolling hills, he saw rocky slopes and craggy mountains.

On they walked, the prisoners staring with glazed eyes at the countryside. A short distance from the bridge, the column passed a stately stone house set well back from the road, surrounded by gardens bright with autumn blossoms. Two young boys were coming down its long pathway walking a dog on a leash.

Suddenly a flurry of brown-and-black fur hurtled through the air and threw itself upon Ross, black paws on his chest, pink tongue on his cheek, and an almost human cry issuing from its throat.

Tam! Ross flung his arms about the dog, holding him in a tight embrace, thankful for the collie's face close to his own and hiding in part the tears that coursed down his cheeks.

The column slowed. Eyes that had been dull with despair brightened at the sight of the dog.

Sternly Ross checked his tears. He wanted no English guard to see him weeping. But when he tried to speak in a soothing tone to quiet Tam, his voice broke. As his vision cleared, he saw that Tam's body had filled out, that his coat was sleek and shining, and that he wore a finely worked leather collar and braided leash.

The two boys came running. The smaller one was fair of coloring, wearing a blue suit that matched his round eyes. "Thomas. Here, Thomas!" he coaxed.

The older boy, dark-haired and thin-faced, halted, dismay upon his face as he looked at Tam and Ross. "There he is. There's Thomas," he faltered.

The younger boy saw only the dog. He started toward Tam and said with an attempt at authority, "Thomas, come here, sir."

Tam looked at the boy and smiled, wagging his tail. He was pressed so close to his master's knees that Ross could feel the taut body trembling.

A guard strode up. "Keep moving there," he ordered, and lifted his foot as if to kick Tam.

Ross held the dog fast, his mind working with lightning speed. He fought down a wild impulse to break into a run and dash across the fields with Tam at his side. But every soldier held a loaded musket. In seconds a score of trained marksmen would fire at him.

In the next moment Ross made his decision. A more cruel one he hoped never to have to make. Every fiber in him longed to keep Tam at his side, but the utter futility of such a wish was as plain as the feel of the dog's fur in his fingers.

Were he to let Tam follow him now, the collie would constantly have to hide from the guards. Even if he succeeded in staying near Ross for the remainder of the march, there was no way he could get aboard the ship that would take the Scots to London. He might take up vigil on the dock, waiting for his master to return. Ross could imagine him growing more lean and wasted daily, watching faithfully for one whom he would nevermore see.

Tam's low growl prompted Ross to speak. Looking full at the guard he warned, "Take care how you treat the pet of these young gentlemen. If I be no' mistaken, their father is a person of consequence."

The guard peered at the boys. The younger one was reaching out a confident hand toward Tam. The older one regarded Ross with a beseeching gaze. He's no fool, thought Ross. He understands that Tam is my dog.

Stooping, Ross put his lips to Tam's ear. "Ye maun go wi' these lads," he ordered hoarsely. "Ye maun stay wi' them. Stay, I tell ye."

He lifted the leash and gestured to the older boy. "Come and get your dog, lad," he said.

The guard moved on, repeating his order to resume march.

Tam must have sensed the urgency in Ross's voice. He stood quietly and allowed the boy to take the lead. But when he felt the pressure of the lad's tug, the collie jerked the leash free and rolled frantic eyes to Ross. Must I go? his agonized gaze seemed to ask. Must I leave you just when I have found you again?

Ross clenched his jaw. He must not let his voice betray his pain. Again he gave the order. "Stay wi' the lad, Tam. He is yer master now."

The dog quivered, then stood quiet. Ross put the leash back in the older boy's hand and laid his own over it. "Care well for this dog, and he will gie his life for ye. Do ye treat him ill—" Ross paused at the fright in the boy's face. No wonder. He must be a fearsome sight with his unkempt hair and tattered plaid. "I know ye'll ne'er do ill to him," he said, then added, "Tam is the name he knows. Ye'd do well to call him that."

The younger boy blurted, "Can we keep him?"

"If we take good care of him," the elder said gravely. He

started back toward the house, and this time Tam followed, though with drooping head and tail.

Ross walked on, staring ahead with sightless eyes, his throat and chest one vast ache. He had thought he was beyond all hurt, that every feeling had long since withered. But the parting from Tam cut deep into his heart. In saying farewell to Tam he knew that he had taken leave of the last vestige of his youth.

All through the day the ragged column moved forward at as rapid a pace as the prisoners could maintain. On either side ranged soldiers who watched the captives with hawk-like ferocity.

At nightfall, when the Scots reached Newcastle-upon-Tyne, they were marched to a quay at the river's edge and herded aboard a ship. It sailed at dawn for London.

Desperate
Venture

Of the voyage down the eastern coast of England the Scots knew little. Shut in the hold for the entire time, they felt every pitch and toss of the vessel. The cramped space and lack of ventilation made Durham Cathedral seem almost pleasant in comparison. Many men were violently seasick.

Hating the confinement without light or air or room to move about, Ross sat hunched in a corner, feeling like a trapped animal. His mind, usually so active, seemed to have deadened. He had a strange feeling of anticipation, of waiting for some as yet unknown event to take place. Meanwhile all his senses seemed dulled, as if he were a creature hibernating.

All about him men conjectured on what would be their fate in London. Would they be confined to another prison? Would they be put to work building roads? Or would they be hanged as a warning to any who dared to take up arms against England?

Ross heard the others talking but did not join in with

them. He could feel the expectation growing within him, as if all his energy were gathering for some tremendous effort. Whatever that might be, he could not tell at the moment. But when the time came, he would be ready. Meanwhile he would rest and husband his strength.

One afternoon the rolling of the ship lessened and stilled, the hatch was opened, and the Scots were ordered up on deck. As he emerged, Ross was conscious at first only of the air, cool and bracing, unbelievably refreshing after the sickening odors below.

Although the day was gray and overcast, he thought he had never seen a more beautiful sight than the open sky and broad river, dotted with crafts of all descriptions. Stately barges proceeded on their way, each with a dozen or more oarsmen rowing in perfect rhythm. Small boats skittered about like so many water beetles. Large seagoing vessels tacked in zigzag progress. And on both sides of the river were crowded more buildings than Ross had ever dreamed he would see all together. Church spires and stately domes rose over roofs of thatch, tile, and slate. And over all hung a pall of smoke from countless chimneys.

Ross had little time to look about. The English seemed to be making up now for all the days wasted in their dilatory herding of the Scots southward from Dunbar.

When the last man had scrambled up the ladder onto the open deck, the prisoners were led onto a long wharf that extended far out into the river. A troop of armed soldiers stood guard over them.

An officer in shining buttons and clanking sword addressed the ship's master. "Be these the hundred and fifty Scots consigned to Augustine Walker of the *Unity* for deportation to the Massachusetts Bay Colony?"

"Aye, and a full count there be," the master answered.

His voice was scarcely audible among the gasps and groans that went up from the line of prisoners. Haggard faces contorted in anguish. Sighs issued from throats that for weeks had stifled moans of pain.

"Deportation! It canna be!"

"Massachusetts! That be far across the sea in the New World!"

"Och, we'll ne'er see Scotland nae mair!"

"Rather I had died o' the flux!"

In dumb disbelief Ross heard the fateful sentence. It echoed and re-echoed in his mind, over and over again, like the tolling of a death knell. Deportation to the Massachusetts Bay Colony!

Those few words meant that he would be forever banished from his native land, exiled to a wilderness from which he might never return. How could he face so cruel a fate? It was not possible that he would never again climb Highland crags, swim in the blue waters of Loch Ruich, or enter the halls of Kindonal Castle.

He could see the line ahead of him moving down the quay toward another ship. In consternation Ross noted the neatly painted name—*Unity*. This must be the vessel that would carry him to that unknown land.

Suddenly he knew that he could never endure deportation! Defeat, hunger, privation, and epidemic he had survived. But this ultimate cruelty was more than he could bear.

The forces that had been slowly gathering within him began to swell. He could feel his excitement mounting. All at once he knew what he must do. Escape! He must escape! There was not a second to lose. If he were ever to break away, he must act now.

Frantically Ross looked about. Just ahead on the wharf was a pile of bales and hogsheads which partially blocked the way. Nearby an ancient cart loaded with crates of cackling chickens creaked and wobbled across the uneven planks. As Ross watched, the cart suddenly struck against a piling. The spokes of the worn wheel splintered, the cart jolted askew, and the load crashed onto the wharf. Some of the crates broke open, loosing fowls that fluttered and squawked about in wild confusion.

A guard near Ross stooped to clutch at a fat hen. In that instant Ross exploded into action. Ducking low, he flashed around the pile of freight and crouched at the edge of the quay, hidden between two hogsheads.

Far below the dark waters of the Thames rose in rhythmic swells. A single small fishing boat bobbed a few yards distant, its two occupants busy with their lines.

Should he chance remaining here? Ross had only a moment to wonder. Then he heard running footsteps and a shout, "After that man!" Any instant now he might be discovered.

Flinging off his plaid and bagpipes, Ross swung himself over the edge of the wharf, curved his legs around a piling, and slid downward. With a shock he hit the icy water and sank into it. Fighting the instinctive need to rise, he forced himself even farther below the surface while the cold bit through his clothes with numbing intensity.

When he judged that he had gone deep enough, he began to swim underwater. With luck he might gain enough distance under the wharf to be out of sight of the guards before he had to come up for air.

Air! He dared not think of it. Already his ears were ringing and his lungs near to bursting. He must drive himself on as far beneath the quay as possible. If he could find a piling and come up on its far side, perhaps he would be undetected.

Through the dark waters he strove, using the underwater strokes he had learned as a boy on Loch Ruich. Then he had swum for the sheer sport of it. Now he was swimming for his life.

When his tortured lungs could bear the pressure no longer, he fought for the surface, and cautiously lifted his head.

He scarcely had time to gulp one hasty breath before he submerged again in terror. He had succeeded in swimming well under the wharf, to be sure, but he had not been unnoticed. Bearing down on him was the fishing boat he had seen earlier. One man was rowing. The other stood in the bow, holding a long pole with a metal hook at one end, and shouting, "There he is!"

Desperately Ross fought his way downward through the water. If only he might reach the river's murky depths where he could not be seen. With the last remnant of his strength he struggled to go deeper.

Suddenly cold iron scraped his knee, and a sharp point jabbed through the flesh of his lower leg. He struggled to free himself, but he was caught fast on the metal hook. Every kick increased his torture and drove the hook deeper. Half crazed with pain he was drawn up through the water and hauled roughly over the edge of the boat, as ingloriously as a gaffed halibut.

"Got him!" the boatman shouted triumphantly. Then he put his foot on Ross's ankle, and with a mighty tug wrenched the hook free.

Blood poured from the wound, and Ross knew searing agony. Through eyes half blinded with shock he could see the boatman's evil face come close, then recede, draw near, then fade. Then the sky and the sea began to revolve, he felt himself swinging around and around, and lost contact with reality.

Newcomers
to the *Unity*

As if from a great distance, Ross heard voices. Slowly, very slowly, he regained consciousness. Chilled to the bone and wet through, he lay on bare boards. His left leg surged with pain.

Now he could hear rough shouts, and a hollow tramp of feet like the rumble of thunder. The voices seemed to come closer. Suddenly he could distinguish words.

"You have an interest in the Iron Works, Mr. Becx?" The speaker's tone was loud and ringing, as if he were accustomed to shouting orders.

"Yes, Master Walker, I am one of the Company of Undertakers of the Iron Works in New England. The Iron Master has been plagued by a dearth of laborers, so I bid for this consignment of captives." The words were cool and precise, as if concerning a shipment of cattle or horses. "Highlanders they are, to be shipped across the Atlantic where they'll have no chance to rise in arms again."

"Think you these Scots can be taught the mysteries of iron making? They look a wild lot to me," boomed the captain.

At the word *Scots,* Ross opened his eyes. He was lying on the deck of a vessel, without doubt the *Unity,* and was separated from the two men by not more than a yard or two. At first he could see only their footgear—one pair of smooth, well-fitting shoes polished to a high lustre, and beside them two sturdy boots covered with white-rimmed salt-water stains. As his gaze roved upward, Ross noted that the man shod in fine leather was richly dressed. His face was pale and cold, with a square black beard. The man in the boots wore plain, practical clothing. Sun and wind had faded the blue of his coat, and bronzed his skin.

"Let the Iron Master concern himself as to their ability." The black-bearded man's words were as cold as his face. "So they be well and sound is all I care."

Beyond the two men Ross could see the line of captives coming on board the vessel, urged on by the guards. If a man stumbled, he was dealt a blow. By what stretch of the imagination could these staggering skeletons be termed well and sound? As in a dream Ross watched the prisoners begin their descent of a ladder in the open hatch and disappear from sight, one by one.

Suddenly one of the polished shoes prodded him in the ribs. "What of this fellow here?" asked Mr. Becx. "Do you mean to take him, or will you feed him to the river rats?"

Ross lay in a half stupor, aware that his life hung in the balance, but too weak and too proud to plead for mercy. If he were cast into the river he would have no hope of survival. With his torn leg he could not swim. But what did anything matter now, whether he drowned in this English river or was transported across the sea? He had lost his last chance to return to Scotland. With it had gone his last hope.

"Be I not mistaken, our agreement, when duly signed, will bind me to carry one hundred and fifty men to Boston," the captain said with slow deliberation. "Be there breath in him when we set sail, he will go with the others. If not, 'twill be an easy matter to heave him overboard."

I'm no more to him than a cask of beef, thought Ross. Should I die, I'll be jettisoned with no more thought than so much spoiled meat. He lay unmoving, feeling as remote and detached as if this were not he, but some other young man who was awaiting the moment of departure and his fate.

"Will all these men go to the Iron Works at Lynn?" inquired the captain.

"Some sixty will be sent there to labor for seven years. The remainder will be bound out for a like term to serve whomsoever shall purchase their time."

Seven years, thought Ross dully. That was almost one quarter of an average man's lifetime.

"Seven years is a fair term," Master Walker said. "I have taken over many an indentured man and maid to labor that length of time in payment for their passage." He paused a moment, then inquired, "You have visited the Iron Works and the village of Hammersmith?"

"Visited that *wilderness?*" Mr. Becx laughed in ridicule. "Indeed not, nor have I the intent to. So the iron makes a profit is my only concern."

All at once Ross felt a tightness in his chest. He coughed, and some of the water that he had swallowed rose in his throat. Gagging, he vomited. The effort cleared his head of some of its fogginess. He struggled to raise himself on one elbow.

"Aha, he's come to," the captain said. His tone was even, betraying neither satisfaction nor displeasure.

"Then we can sign the papers—for the full number," Mr. Becx said.

"They are in my cabin. Shall we attend to that matter now?" The captain's tone was brusque.

"Should you not have that man put below with the others? He might attempt to escape," Mr. Becx suggested.

The captain gave an impatient snort. "He can do no harm where he is."

"Unbound? Those Highlanders are a tough lot."

"I scarce think it necessary," muttered the captain. But he ordered a crewman, "Lash this man to the rail." Then he and Mr. Becx walked through a low doorway to the captain's cabin.

Rough hands seized Ross. Two sailors jerked him upright, dragged him to the side of the ship, and sat him down with his back against the rail. Then they bound him, pulling the ropes tight across his chest and arms. Looking down he could see a red stain spreading on the boards beneath his torn leg. Again he vomited.

In a short time the last of the Scots had been driven below decks. Sailors had placed a covering over the hatch and were battening it down when Master Walker and Mr. Becx emerged from the cabin.

"You are a practical man, sir," Mr. Becx remarked, his tone oily with approbation. "I trust that your voyage will be speedy and that its conclusion will prosper us both." He showed his teeth in a grimace intended for a smile, crossed over the gangplank, walked pompously down the wharf, and climbed into a waiting carriage.

Master Walker threw a swift glance at the small boats on the river, then at a pennant flying from a tower. "Make ready to cast off," he bawled.

Sailors began rushing about in what seemed unutterable confusion. Some climbed up the ratlines to the spars, others busied themselves with the myriad ropes that ran from the rigging to the deck.

Drifting between awareness and insensibility, Ross sagged against the rough planks, his head tilted back, and his gaze fastened on the city in bitter regret. If only he had been able to get away, he might even now be hiding somewhere among those crowded buildings.

At the far end of the quay, two figures came into view, hurrying toward the *Unity*. Ross could see that one was a thin, well-dressed gentleman and the other a slender young girl who half walked, half ran at his side, lifting the folds of her peacock-blue cloak.

Ross jerked to full consciousness, blinking in disbelief. They could not be the same. Not the father and daughter who had fled over the Elvet Bridge. Such a coincidence might take place in a tale or ballad, but never in the world of fact.

As the two drew near enough for him to make out their faces, he knew that his eyes were not playing him false. The man was indeed the gentleman he had seen before, and the girl was none other than the one called Joanna.

The gentleman raised his arm and called out to Master Walker, "Hold! We seek passage on your vessel."

Ross listened incredulously. The girl and her father had succeeded in escaping from the Roundheads. They had made their way to London, and now—

The sailors assigned to haul in the gangplank paused in their work.

"I've but one cabin, and I cannot wait for your luggage to be brought." There was dismissal in the master's tone.

The man turned to his daughter questioningly. She smiled at him, as if in assent.

"We will take the cabin. And you need not wait for luggage." There was urgency in the voice—authority, too.

"You can pay?" asked Walker.

In reply the man held up a gold coin.

"Come aboard, then."

The man stood aside, gesturing the girl ahead. Ross noted

the quick look she gave to the city, as if in farewell. Then she squared her shoulders, lifted her head, and with determined tread, stepped across the gangplank. Her father hurried after and began to converse with Master Walker.

All at once, it seemed, sails were unfurled, and lines cast off. The *Unity* began to move.

After one swift glance toward Ross, the girl took a stand at the rail across from him. She was not looking back at the crowded city now, nor at the green hills. Her gaze was straight ahead, down the river, and beyond.

Motionless she stood there, her slender body wrapped in the velvet cloak, her head high, as beautiful as a peacock, and as aloof. Ross was certain that she did not even know that he existed.

The captain and the Englishman stood near Ross. "As soon as we are well under way I shall have my necessaries brought up to the charthouse, Mr. Sprague. Then you and your daughter may take possession of my cabin." Master Walker's tone was gruff.

"Perchance this may make the imposition less onerous," Mr. Sprague said in a placating tone. He slipped a coin into the other man's hand.

"Quite so," replied the master. One corner of his mouth turned up, and his eyes brightened. Then he climbed to the poop deck and began shouting commands.

Ross could feel the vessel gaining momentum. Above his head the sails filled with wind and billowed out. The world was a maze of canvas and hempen lines and scurrying figures.

In a daze Ross watched while two of the crew carried a chest and a roll of bedding up to the charthouse that opened off the quarter-deck. He saw Mr. Sprague escort his daughter to the doorway of the newly vacated cabin and return to meet the captain as he climbed down to the main deck.

"May I inquire, Master Walker, why you keep one of your crew thus bound?" The gentleman gestured toward Ross.

"One of my crew? Hah, that is but a portion of my cargo."

"Your cargo? I do not understand your meaning. Or do you jest?"

"A hundred and a half Scots are in the 'tween decks, sir. Taken by Cromwell, they were, at Dunbar. He dared not turn them loose lest they take up arms again, and to keep them in prison would be costly. So he's turned a profit instead by deporting them to Massachusetts."

"Poor devils!" said Mr. Sprague.

"They're better off here than rotting in gaol," the captain said.

"And this man?" The Englishman gestured toward Ross.

"A fool who sought to escape at the last minute. With guards on every side he'd no more chance than a herring in a flock of gulls."

The gentleman looked at the receding city and widening

river as if measuring the distance from the ship to land. "Would you not think it safe to unbind him now?" he asked.

"I'll see to it presently," the captain said carelessly.

"You'd have no objection to my loosening his bonds?"

The captain shrugged. "As you wish," he said, and walked off.

Mr. Sprague moved carefully across the tilting deck. Kneeling at Ross's side, he began to work at the knots. Although slender, his fingers were strong.

How long since anybody but his own comrades had shown Ross kindness? Surely this could not be happening to him.

Mr. Sprague was muttering in anger. "If one of my grooms had treated a horse thus I'd have sent him packing." He loosened the knot, pulled the ends of the rope free, and unwound the coils from Ross's body. Then he turned his attention to Ross's leg.

As he examined the wound, Mr. Sprague sucked in his breath. Ross looked again at the torn flesh, and felt his head reeling.

"Master Walker must have some ointments and lint for dressings, but I'll not wait for those," the Englishman said. "I'll bind this now as best I can."

He drew a large linen handkerchief from his pocket, and ripped it in half. On each side of the torn calf he laid a folded piece of the clean linen. Then he removed his coat, and with a small knife slashed off a long strip of lining. This he wrapped around the leg.

Although the pain was intense, Ross clamped his jaw resolutely. He had endured so much, he must not break down now and give in like a weakling.

Such kindness was deserving of more than ordinary thanks. How could he convey his gratitude suitably? He was grappling with words, and had begun, "I gie ye my thanks, sir . . ." when of a sudden the world went blank, and he knew no more.

A Way
Out

In a fragmented nightmare Ross tossed and turned. His whole frame was in torment, a vast ache that emanated from the core of fire that burned in his leg.

Suddenly he found himself bound to a stake in Tantallon's courtyard with flames leaping and licking at his body. Beside him stood Kettie, her dark eyes wild with fright and pain while the fire raced up the skirt of her gown.

Ross tried to scream for help, but no sound came. He attempted to wrench himself out of the bonds that held him fast, but could not move. Then he made one mighty effort to free himself, and felt as if he had torn his leg apart.

The next moment he was in his childhood bed in Kindonal Castle. The Laird sat beside him, stroking his head with his long, thin fingers. "There, there." His tone was tender and comforting. "Have no fear. 'Tis all past now."

Trembling, Ross clung to the cool fingers, knowing the

peace of homecoming. He was safe in Kindonal. The fire
and the stake were naught but a dream.

Then he seemed to float up and away from the castle,
and all at once he was on the bridge at Berwick. Below him
a seal looked up with mocking glance, while he struggled
to make his way to the river Tweed and drink of the water
that was so near and so inviting. He tried to move, but could
not, and looking down, saw that he was held fast to the
stonework by an iron bolt that pierced his leg. Again he
opened his mouth to cry out, but could make not even a
whisper.

Miraculously, in an instant, he was back in Kindonal, and
the Laird was holding a cup to his lips. The cup was of
silver; he knew its thin edge well. He drank deeply, and
again felt the release from fear. He was safe in his own
bed, and the Laird was close by. Naught could harm him
here.

Without warning the scene shifted. He was on Doon Hill
in the watery dawn, with the English cavalry charging the
right flank, driving the Scottish horse down upon its foot
soldiers. Ross struggled to draw his claymore, but the sword
stuck fast in its scabbard. At that instant an English soldier
struck at him with leveled halberd and stabbed it into his
leg. He could feel the shock of the weapon's thrust as it
bit deep into the flesh. He tried to call out for help, for
mercy, but his throat seemed paralyzed. The next moment
he was beaten to the ground under a rain of death-dealing
hoofs.

Ross woke to darkness and the rasp of snores. The air reeked with the sour smell of men's unwashed bodies. He lay shaking, and soaked in sweat. Where might he be? In the guard room at Tantallon? No, the torch that burned all night outside the doorway there was missing.

Was he in the cathedral? His fingers touched the boards beneath him. No, these were not the straw and stones of Durham.

From above came the tramp of feet and the creak of ropes. He recognized the odor of tar, and knew that he was on a vessel. He had left Newcastle and was on the way to London. Soon he and his comrades would learn what their fate might be.

Suddenly full realization flooded over him. He was on a ship bound for America and servitude. Moreover, his leg was hurt and useless. From the depths of his misery he gave a deep groan.

Beside him there was the stirring of a large body. Ross felt a hand touch his cheek, gentle for all its size. Then he heard Duncan Muir say, "Yer fever's gone, lad. May the Lord be thankit!" His voice broke in what sounded like a sob.

Ross tried to say his friend's name, but only a whisper came from his throat. He attempted to lift his hand to clap Duncan on the shoulder, but he could barely move his fingers.

"Ye'll be needin' water," Duncan said, and vanished. A grunting and heaving ensued as he made his way between sleeping men. A few minutes later he returned, carrying a wooden bucket.

Supporting Ross's head, Duncan held the thick rim to his lips. "Take a sip o' this," he urged.

Ross obeyed, but the water ran from his slack lips after the first swallow.

"That be enow," Duncan said. "Here's a bit o' biscuit I've been savin' against this time. Do ye suck on it, ye may feel better come the morn."

The ship's bread was as hard as iron and about as tasty. Ross let it fall from his grasp. Beneath him the deck rose and fell with each pitch and toss of the vessel. It was hard to distinguish the movement of the ship from the heaving of his stomach and the dizziness in his head. There was a dull ache in his torn leg that presaged agony should he move it.

Scarcely hearing the groans and wheezes of the closely packed men around him, Ross sank deep into his own misery. He had failed in his last-minute attempt at escape. And through his own folly he had suffered an injury that could mean the loss of his leg—or worse. He had never known such complete despair.

One by one he rehearsed the tragic train of events that had led to his incarceration in this pitching vessel, the nightmare that had begun when the clan was called to arms. Why had he been such a fool as to listen to those brave songs of battle? Why had he not heeded the Laird's counsel and remained at Kindonal?

He began to count his losses. First was the Laird, dead of a fever. Next was Black Donald, slain in battle. Both men Ross had loved with a deep devotion, though to neither had he dared admit his feeling. The Laird's high position had set an unseen barrier between them and stifled any word of affection from Ross. And the fear of Black Donald's scorn had kept Ross from ever voicing his admiration of his father.

And there was Kettie. He had unwittingly led her to her death. Had he not helped her away from Tantallon, she might still be within its strong walls, and alive. A shudder of regret passed through him. If only he had been able to escape and find refuge in that fortress!

He thought of men who had died in battle, and those who had fallen on the march. There were many who had died of the flux, Dougal among them. He had been a good lad, too young to lose his life when he had such a hearty appetite for living.

The memory of Tam flashed through his mind. For a moment Ross could feel the rasp of the dog's tongue on his cheek, hear his eager panting, and grasp the thick fur of his coat. There had never been a dog more faithful. And he had repaid that devotion by abandoning the collie.

In all the dark picture only one bright ray shone. That was the remembrance of Hugh's escape from Durham in the cassock Ross had given him, by means of the plan Ross had conceived. Yet even here despair crept into Ross's mind. There was no guarantee of Hugh's safety after he left the cathedral. It could be he had been speared by an English soldier ere he was halfway to the Border.

As for himself, he had lost every prospect for the future. If it were not for the war, he might now be at the Laird's right hand in Kindonal, learning how to govern. Or he might be striding forward with his father, piping a march to stir up the clan. Now he would never again see the Highland hills for which his heart cried out.

If only he could go back and relive the past few months! Not again would he be lured into taking up arms. Nevermore would he march away from his native hills.

The whole campaign had been a massive blunder, and his part in it a series of mistakes. At Dunbar he had not been able to strike one blow for Scotland and the Covenant. On the march there had been a few chances for escape, but each time he had fumbled them miserably—either lacked the daring to make the break, or had let a friend go in his stead. How could he have been so stupid?

Now the English were overrunning Scotland, eating grain that had been planted for Scots, feeding on sheep and cattle raised for Highlanders, living in their homes, and roaming their hills. Not only that, but they had banished the true owners of Scottish lands to exile, and as a bitter finale, were profiting by the sale of their captives.

Deportation was an inhuman thing—but selling men as slaves—surely that was the ultimate cruelty! No men on earth valued their freedom more than Highlanders, nor relinquished it with more pain and reluctance.

As Ross lay in the blackness, immersed in misery, an idea entered his mind that was so magnificent that it gave his spirits a momentary lift. Quite unintentionally he had stumbled upon a way in which he could thoroughly cheat the English. It was the only means remaining to him by which he could avenge the wrongs he had suffered. His triumph would be bitter, but it would be complete. He would take the one escape route still open to him—the doorway into death.

To die would not be difficult. Indeed, it would be simpler than making the effort necessary for survival. His body was so wasted that little reserve remained. A few days of hunger, a few more days of thirst, and the slight pulse of his life would slow to a halt. Then there would be one less Scot whose labors would serve to swell British coffers.

Now he had something to look forward to, a goal to work toward. Ross felt around on the deck for the biscuit that Duncan had given him, and tried to throw it. His attempt was feeble, but effective enough. A minute later he heard the gnawing of a rat and its rapid swallowing, and knew that the rodent had found the biscuit. The knowledge filled him with a grim satisfaction.

Unwanted
Advice

In the morning streaks of light showed through cracks between the planking overhead. The prisoners crowded around Ross. He discovered that he had achieved a certain importance during the days he had lain unconscious while his wound festered and his fever mounted.

"Ye'd be dead now, were it no' for Mr. Sprague," said Duncan. "Yer leg was as big as a barrel, and ye were fair out o' yer head. He came to see ye each day, and yester morn when he saw that ye were worse, he took his wee knife and stabbed it into the swellin'. Och, but ye should hae seen the poison run out. And that verra nicht yer fever broke."

Ross put a tentative hand on his bound leg. It was tender to his touch, but the wracking pain was gone. Only a dull, persistent ache remained. He could endure that for the brief time remaining. In a day or two he would be free of everything—of pain, regret, loneliness, and that engulfing sense of failure and emptiness. And the English would be cheated of their profit. He would triumph over them after all!

"Ye look a bit mair braw, lad," Duncan said. "It must be frae the biscuit ye ate in the nicht."

Ross lowered his eyelids. Deceiving Duncan was the only part of the plan he disliked, but it was necessary if he was to be successful.

In the middle of the morning a sudden shaft of light pierced the gloom of the 'tween decks area, and a draft of cool wind stirred the sour odors. A sailor leaned down through a square opening and bellowed an order. The Scots crowded to the ladder that led upward.

Duncan lingered beside Ross. " 'Tis time for our airing. We be let up on deck each day to stretch our legs and fill our lungs wi' the good salt air. Can ye get alang by yersel'?" There was eager impatience in every word.

"Aye, dinna fash yersel' o'er me," Ross answered, and Duncan hurried to a place at the foot of the ladder.

A short time after the last Scot had vanished through the opening, Mr. Sprague's elegantly clothed lower limbs appeared, then the rest of his body, descending the ladder.

When the older man leaned over Ross, his lined face filled with relief. "So, young man, you are mending, and none the worse for my ministrations." He drew forth a silver flask. "If you will drink some of this, it will strengthen you." He raised Ross's head and tilted the bottle.

Ross could feel the liquor on his lips, and was tempted.

But his determination to take no nourishment was fresh and strong, and he kept his mouth tightly closed. If Mr. Sprague had not meddled, thought Ross, I'd be dead by now, forever free of this accursed bondage.

For a moment Mr. Sprague's thin fingers brushed his cheek. Ross could have sworn it was the Laird's hand. He almost weakened. It would be easy to give in to this man's care, to accept whatever comfort might come his way. But then he would be playing into English hands, and living to labor for an English master for seven endless years.

Mustering all his will, Ross shook off the ministering touch and closed his eyes, partly in dismissal, partly to shut out the hurt on the lined face.

For a brief space Mr. Sprague sat in silence. Then he rose slowly. "You seem to be less well than I had hoped," he said. "I shall look in on you tomorrow." He walked across the tilting deck and mounted the ladder.

Duncan had returned in time to witness Ross's silent rebuff. He burst out impatiently, "What ails ye, lad, that ye should treat the man so? When ye were out o' yer senses ye clung to his hands as if he were yer only friend. Aye, an' ye called him the Laird."

So those cool fingers and the soothing voice that had comforted him had not been entirely a dream. Ross pushed the memory away. He would not soften now.

All that day Ross kept to his resolution. When offered water he locked his lips. The salt beef and biscuit that

Duncan tried to feed him he refused. His one worry was that Duncan might guess his purpose. But the huge Highlander seemed unaware of his intent.

"Had I a bit o' broth or some oatcake e'en, ye might eat. 'Tis no wonder ye hae no stomach fer this slop."

That night Ross could feel his strength ebbing. The next day he drifted off into long periods of semiconsciousness.

At mid-morning while the prisoners were on deck, Mr. Sprague descended the ladder. He offered his flask, and again Ross shook his head in denial. The older man felt Ross's forehead. Ross quivered at the touch, and closed his eyes. It was all he could do not to weep at the memories stirred by those long, slim fingers. Then Mr. Sprague spoke.

"I know what is in your mind. Think you not but that others may have had the same thoughts?"

Ross lifted his head in astonishment.

"How can ye tell what I think?" he asked.

Mr. Sprague gave Ross a piercing look. For the first time Ross detected the depths of suffering in his eyes. "Because I, too, have had just such thoughts and have been sorely tempted to take the same way out that you now seek."

"Then let me go my ain way, and dinna try to hold me back," Ross said angrily.

The Englishman flinched as if he had been struck. "Forgive me for attempting to interfere with your plans," he said with stiff formality. "I should have remembered that the young have interest in none but themselves and will take aught but counsel from their elders."

He rose and unbuttoned his coat to put the flask in an inside pocket. As the garment fell open, Ross could see the slashed lining. He regarded the ragged cloth malevolently. He had not asked for the Englishman's help. At the same time he could not suppress a stab of guilt. The day that he lay trussed on the deck with blood pouring from his wound he had been thankful enough for Mr. Sprague's care. He knew that he should say some word of gratitude now, but his lips felt leaden, and he remained silent. Then Mr. Sprague was gone, without a backward glance in his direction.

Ross lay back on the planks, his mind churning. If only Mr. Sprague had left him alone! He had been content enough before; his resolution had been firm. Why must he now be troubled by the words of this fugitive Englishman?

Fragments of his conversation with Mr. Sprague returned to torment Ross. What circumstance had caused so fine a gentleman to wish to take his own life? Though he had not said it in so many words, that had been his meaning, Ross was sure. Even more tormenting was the question that followed: What had kept the Englishman from carrying out his purpose?

Ross tried to regain his former single-mindedness by picturing the chagrin that the captain would feel when he discovered that part of his cargo had slipped from his grasp. Though he turned the thought over and over in his mind, it was losing its savor, like a sweetmeat held too long on the tongue. Doubtless his fatigue and weakness were responsible. Soon, however, they would take complete control of his body and mind, and he would have to struggle no more with either hunger or conscience.

From time to time during the day a prisoner would approach Ross and attempt to feed him a bit of meat or a piece of hardtack saved from his own scant allotment. Others offered water. Stubbornly Ross refused all nourishment, and at length they left him alone. Only Duncan remained nearby, his face a mask of anxiety.

The third day after his fever had broken, Ross had difficulty in awakening. The borderline between reality and unconsciousness was growing hazy. He had a question in his mind, but the recalling of it took effort. It was something about Mr. Sprague. Ah, yes. Why had he turned away from his wish to die?

For hours Ross lay waiting for the square of brightness that would signal the Scots' time of egress and the Englishman's descent into the 'tween decks. Finally he could bear the suspense no longer, and asked weakly, "Mr. Sprague— will he no' come?"

Duncan was hunched nearby. "Ye canna think he would come back after ye answered him sae sairly?"

Ross mulled over the words. Dimly he could recall confessing to Duncan his rejection of the Englishman's kindnesses, the greatest of them the sharing of his private anguish. The memory served to sharpen his need. He must learn what had caused Mr. Sprague to change his purpose.

"I maun ask him ane wee thing," he said painfully.

Duncan's face worked in pity. "Ye'd best gie up the thocht, lad. I dinna think he will come again."

Ross put all his strength into his next words. "Could ye nae tell him that I maun sec him ane time more?"

Duncan gave a great sigh and heaved to his feet. He made his way to the ladder, climbed up a step, and rapped on the door overhead.

It opened, and a sailor put his face to the opening. "Are you ready to hand up the corpse?" he asked.

"Nay, there's breath in him yet," Duncan answered. "He would see Mr. Sprague again."

The trap door fell with a loud clap. Then there was darkness and silence broken by a murmuring among the prisoners. Ross lay weakly, his breath coming in short gasps. It seemed as if the scant remnants of his vitality were focussed on the question that filled his mind. To it was now added another. Had the Englishman received his message, and if so, would he comply with the request of one who had treated him so ill?

A few minutes later the trap door creaked upward, and Mr. Sprague appeared. In a white heat of impatience Ross waited. Then the lined face bent over him, and the cool, dry voice said, "You wished to have a word with me?"

The Englishman had made no mention of yesterday, nor of Ross's rejection of him. His generosity gave Ross courage. "When ye thocht on it, why did ye no' do it?" he asked.

Mr. Sprague understood, as Ross had known he would. His face darkened, and for one terrible moment Ross feared he might not answer. Then he said slowly, in a voice so low that only Ross could hear, "I could tell from your talk when you were wandering in your mind that you had known some love and tenderness in your childhood. I, too, was fortunate, perchance more so, for I had devoted parents, then a loving wife, and a child now grown to womanhood. All would have gone well for me and my family except for my allegiance to my sovereign. When my activities in his behalf became suspect, some weeks past, I was forced to bring my daughter and my wife, then gravely ill of a fever, to my parents' home for safety. My dear wife was weakened by the rigors of the journey, and died in three days' time. We were at her funeral service when Cromwell's soldiers attacked the chapel."

"Not the chapel!" Ross could only whisper the words.

"Yes, the chapel. My ears may never be free of the ring of the steel as it splintered the windows," Mr. Sprague said in a choked voice. "My father pushed Joanna through a side door, and insisted that I follow. I knew that I should remain to defend him and my mother, but I was still dazed by the death of my wife. My father was strong in body as well as spirit, and for years I had deferred to him. Joanna and I made our way unseen to the stables, mounted two horses, and got safely away."

The Englishman let his head fall forward in his hands. After a moment he lifted his face and continued, "I could not forgive myself for my cowardly flight, and I cannot even now. When I learned that both my parents had been killed by Cromwell's men, my guilt was so burdensome that I was certain I could bear it no longer. So I decided to end my life."

Ross could feel his impatience bursting its bonds. "And why did ye no' do so?" he demanded.

Again Mr. Sprague hesitated, then inquired slowly, "You have been brought up a Christian?"

"Aye."

"I am not well acquainted with the Scottish kirk, but doubtless your service makes some provision for the absolution of sin. In our English prayer book is a section that begins: 'Almighty God, the Father of our Lord Jesus Christ, who desireth not the death of a sinner, but rather that he may turn from his wickedness and live. . . .' " Mr. Sprague repeated the words slowly, with deep meaning. "I could not get those words out of my mind. Night and day they echoed in my thoughts, until I knew that I must not die, especially not by my own hand, but that I must turn from my wickedness and *live*."

Ross looked full into the deepset eyes. "It couldna hae been easy."

"No, it was very difficult. But once made, the decision seemed right and proper. You understand that had I taken my own life, Joanna might have fallen into enemy hands, and then my parents' sacrifice would have been in vain. Their hope was to save the last of the line."

Ross was silent. What was there to say? In his mind's eye he could see a fine estate such as those he had passed on the Great Road. He could picture Mr. Sprague with his wife and daughter moving through gracious rooms, seated before a fire, or gathered about a dinner table. He could see a mourning family and servants gathered in the chapel, and feel their terror at the untimely Roundhead attack. In his own heart he could sense the frantic fear of a father for a daughter such as Joanna. What would he himself have done in such a case?

Ross remembered the agony he had known on beholding Black Donald dead on the field of battle. How much greater would have been his pain had he deserted his father at the time of the enemy's attack. Surely Mr. Sprague had suffered cruelly. Not only had he lost wife and parents, and the landed estate and fortune that had been his birthright, but he would always know the torment of his special guilt.

Ross drew a deep, shuddering breath. He summoned strength to lift his hand enough to touch that of the Englishman. It was the only comfort he could manage.

To his dismay Mr. Sprague pulled his hand away, and eyed Ross sternly. "You are not fool enough to believe I told you all this to arouse your pity? No, my intent was—" He stopped. "I might as well save my breath."

Ross felt his courage ebbing beneath the forceful gaze. He could almost guess at the older man's purpose, but in his weakness his mind worked but slowly.

All at once the Englishman's face softened. "Do you not understand what I am trying to tell you?" he asked. "You Scots are not the only ones to have suffered. Others have met even worse fates. Consider the English Royalists, and the thousands of Irish who were slaughtered. Then you may be thankful that you have still your life and a future."

"A future?" Ross croaked scornfully, instantly on the defensive. "What future can there be in deportation?"

"What is my own voyage but deportation?" countered Mr. Sprague. "Think you I can return to an England under Cromwell?"

Did Mr. Sprague think that he could break down a Scot's determination so easily? Desperately Ross clung to his grievances. "But indenture for seven years!" he pursued stubbornly.

"In seven years you will be but at your prime," argued the Englishman. "What I would not give for such a boon!"

Ross could think of no further argument. His brain felt foggy, and no matter what he might say he was sure that this keen, intelligent man would parry his thrust. For the moment he was too tired to care about anything but the need for rest.

Weakness overcame him. Wearily he let his eyelids fall, and sank into sleep. Perhaps this time he would slip through the doorway that led to death.

Black
Donald

How long he had slept, Ross did not know, but suddenly he was once more in the grip of a dream, terrifying in its reality. He was on a vast moor in the mists of a gray dawn. Behind him in the gloaming straggled the men of Kindonal, gaunt ghosts with scarcely the strength to drag one foot after another. Far ahead in the distance loomed the shadowy outline of Tantallon. Its lofty towers seemed to beckon through the enshrouding murk.

Suddenly from the Scots' rear ranks came a cry of terror. Looking back, Ross could see a band of English soldiers approaching, their coats red and their weapons jangling.

Ross knew with a dreadful certainty that there was only one way for the exhausted captives to save themselves. They must flee to the stronghold of Tantallon! He also knew that at their present tortoise-like pace they could never reach its ramparts in time. Only if he could pipe some life into their wearied bodies might they gain its walls.

With one quick movement he swung the bagpipes into

position. In a frenzied filling and emptying of his lungs he blew air into the sheepskin. The bag taut under his left arm, his fingers on the chanter, he jerked his elbow inward with a strong thrust for a mighty rallying note.

To his dismay, no sound came forth! With a tremendous effort he tried again to squeeze air from the sheepskin. Not a wheeze or a whine issued from the pipes.

After a third futile attempt, while panic rose in his throat, he saw a gigantic form marching toward him from out of the gray light. It was his father!

Near to exploding in one of the towering rages that had earned him his name, Black Donald bore down upon Ross like an avenging fury, the drones of his bagpipes rising weapon-like over his shoulder. His wild bellow rang out across the moor.

"How can ye hope to pipe spirit into men's souls if ye've nae spirit within yersel'? Fer all ye're me ain bluid, ye're nae but a pukin' milksop, and I'll no' claim kinship wi' ye nae mair." Then he struck at the bagpipes in Ross's grasp, and roared in a voice like the Last Judgment, "It takes a man wi' heart to pipe the clan where they maun go, and ye're no' fit to wheedle a warble frae the warpipes!"

With that he loosed a violent burst of music from the instrument he carried. The song shattered the bonds of fatigue and discouragement that had paralyzed the Scots. With new energy they dashed forward to the castle, outdistancing the English.

But Ross could only stumble after, frozen by his own

failure, sickened by his father's contempt. When he reached Tantallon, the last of the Scots had passed under the rapidly descending portcullis. Ross tried to follow, but the draw-bridge rattled up just out of his reach, and he tottered on the edge of the moat while the bright swords of the English drew nearer and ever nearer.

He woke to the sound of his own screams. For a few minutes he lay panting in terror, waiting for the touch of the Laird's cool fingers, his low reassurances.

Then Duncan's face floated above his own.

"Tantallon," breathed Ross. "I couldna get inside."

"Small guid it would hae done ye," said Duncan bitterly. "There's nae wall built but will fall to Cromwell."

"He could ne'er ding doon Tantallon," whispered Ross.

"An' has he no' dinged doon e'en mightier castles?" Duncan asked in dour severity. "There's naught can stand against yon fiend."

The fringes of the dream still fluttered in Ross's mind. He could see the English hauling cannon and great batter-ing rams near Tantallon, and aiming their deadly shots at its walls. With a sickening clarity he realized that Dun-can was right. No stronghold was safe from Cromwell and his men.

The knowledge was unnerving. Painfully he relinquished his vision of Tantallon as a final refuge, and at that moment, he was seized by a vast tremor. His whole body was racked by a shivering so violent that he could not control it.

" 'Tis the weakness that brings on sich chittering," Duncan cried.

Weakness? Not that alone. Ross knew what truly caused his trembling. It was terror, pure terror, at the remembrance of his father's words. Even now they echoed and re-echoed in his mind. *Ye're nae but a pukin' milksop, an' I'll no' claim kinship wi' ye nae mair.*

How had Black Donald learned about his inner defeat? How had he known that his son had not the courage to go on living, but had chosen instead to die?

All through his life there had been nothing he longed for so much as his father's approval. His thoughts of death had been the sweeter as he had looked forward to being once more with Black Donald. But always he had pictured them marching together, side by side, their bagpipes skirling in perfect unison. Now that hope was shattered.

Was there no comfort left anywhere, in this life or the next? As he had so often before, Ross started to review the wrongs he had suffered. Strangely enough, the keenness of his injuries now seemed to have dulled. His losses seemed less sharp in comparison with the cruelties wreaked upon the Spragues and others of Cromwell's victims. His own fate seemed less tragic, his future less onerous.

Slowly he took stock of his situation, and as he did so he could hear the breath rasping in his throat. He could feel the regular rise and fall of his chest, and the even beat of his heart. For all he had endured, he was still alive.

Suddenly he almost cried aloud in excitement. Was there not a better way to outwit the English? Had he not discovered, and not a moment too soon, a means of proving the worth of Scottish blood?

He would live! And he would live to prove to the English that they could not completely defeat a true Scot. His family and friends they might kill, his country they might conquer, his freedom they might curtail for seven years or more. But his spirit they could not vanquish! He would prove it.

The echo of his father's words rang again in his ears. *It takes a man wi' heart to pipe the clan where they maun go.* How could he have so far forgotten the weird that was laid on a piper?

Beside him Duncan held out a biscuit. "Ye maun eat, man, an' ye're no' to die," he said sternly.

Ross's trembling hand could scarcely guide the hard bread to his lips. He managed to push it into his mouth and clamped his teeth upon its unyielding surface. Gradually his shivering ceased, and he could lie still. But the bread was too dry for him to chew in his thirsty state.

Ross could see Duncan eyeing him warily. When he took the hardtack from his mouth so that he might speak, the disgust in Duncan's face was almost more than he could bear. He knew then that Duncan had guessed his secret.

He was still too weak to waste words. "Water?" he asked.

In answer Duncan gave a great smile that lit his whole face. But as he held the bucket to Ross's lips, he cautioned,

"Dinna drink o'ermuch lest ye gie yer insides a jolt. An' ye can hae nae mair than the ane bit o' bread."

Ross knew then that all was well between him and Duncan. He gnawed hungrily on the biscuit, and in his famished state, he thought he had never tasted anything more delicious.

Only one worry clouded his mind. In all the days of his illness he had been so concerned with his woes that he had given no thought to his bagpipes. Now he was filled with an overwhelming need to know what had happened to his instrument.

His last remembrance of the pipes was when he had thrown them and his plaid down on the wharf just before he had flung himself into the river Thames. The plaid was covering him now. He would know anywhere the feel of its woolen strands, and the faint scent of heather that he fancied still clung to its worn fibers. Someone, probably Duncan, had picked it up after the ghastly fiasco of his attempted escape. It was too much to hope that his bagpipes had also been saved.

For a long time he lay wrestling with himself. Was it better to remain in doubt? At least he now had a small hope that the pipes were nearby. Yet with every passing moment cold common sense told him that no guard in the world would have allowed a prisoner to pick up and bring on board so useless and so completely Scottish a thing as a set of bagpipes.

Finally he could bear the suspense no longer. Shifting the

piece of hardtack in his mouth, he looked toward Duncan. "Me pipes?" he asked, hardly daring to voice the words. And once they were out, he wished he might recall them, so greatly did he fear the answer.

To his relief, Duncan rose and began burrowing in a crevice between some bales and the hull of the ship. Soon he returned with an awkward bundle Ross recognized.

"Ye've John Davison to thank fer savin' yer things," Duncan said. "He's that wispy he could wrap yer pipes and plaid inside his ain and no' look stouter than the least o' us!"

Cradling the bagpipes in his arms, Ross felt their knobby bulk with a pang of bitter remembrance. He slid his fingers over the polished surface of the drones and chanter with a pleasure that was the keener for the knowledge that he might never have touched them again.

The pipes were a part of his life. He knew that now. But it had been necessary for him almost to lose them forever, as well as the right to play them, before he had appreciated their significance.

A vast humility filled his soul. If only he might be worthy, worthy of the right to pipe, and of the friendship of the men who had made his piping possible.

In greater contentment than he had known for weeks, he lay quietly, waiting for strength to return. In his inmost ear he could hear Black Donald piping a triumphant pibroch, and in his secret eye he could imagine that his father was looking upon him with approval. For the moment he could ask no more.

Piper
to the Clan

Regaining his strength was not so easy as Ross had anticipated. His stomach had been empty for so long that it did
not at first take kindly to the food sent down to it. For
a while he was seized with violent cramps and he began
to doubt the wisdom of his decision. Then Duncan begged
some oats from one of the sailors who brought down the
daily food. He mixed these raw with water to make the
drammock that was the mainstay of hunters in the heather.
The very thought that such fare had nourished numberless
Scots before him made the dish palatable to Ross. His
stomach accepted his dictum, and from that time on he
began to mend.

On the following day Ross looked forward with con-
flicting emotions to the coming of Mr. Sprague. He was
well aware that the Englishman had shown uncommon
kindness to him, and that he had repaid him with crass
ingratitude. Now that he had regained his senses, how
could he face the older man?

For hours, it seemed, he tossed and turned on the hard boards, wondering how to plead forgiveness. When the trap door creaked open, he knew overwhelming panic, and was relieved that Duncan waited until the other captives had gone up on deck.

When Mr. Sprague came down into the 'tween decks, the husky Scot boomed, "Yestreen the lad took a turn for the better. Ye can see fer yersel' that his een are the mair bricht now." Then he climbed to the open deck.

Mr. Sprague knelt beside Ross. "There is no need to ask after your health, young man. It is clear that you are improving. And I perceive another change—of greater import."

"For that I hae ye to thank," said Ross haltingly. "An' I maun beg ye to forgie me for bein' so ingrate these days past."

"What one of us has not said things he would like to forget? Naught matters now save that you are mending. Now, then, let me look at your leg. I have some clean linen here from the captain's store."

Gently Mr. Sprague untied the old bandage, stiff with blood and pus, and bent over the injured limb. Ross kept his eyes averted. Then curiosity prevailed. Steeling himself, he looked down at his calf. After one brief glance, he turned his eyes away in sick disgust. This could not be any part of his body, this purplish mass of swollen flesh.

"Ah, the healing is proceeding more rapidly than I had

expected," Mr. Sprague said, satisfaction evident in every word.

Ross looked down again. Now he could see that the edges of the wound were drawing together, and that a scab was forming.

" 'Twas a mercy that the bone was not affected, else you might have been lamed for life," continued the Englishman. "Now, then, flex your knee a bit."

Every instinct warned him against such action. You will feel pain, an inner voice cried, as Ross forced himself to bend his knee. Pain there was, but not the sharp agony he had known before. This was an ache a man could bear.

"Move your leg about from time to time," suggested Mr. Sprague. "Tomorrow you may wish to stand and take a step or two."

Suddenly Ross was filled with a vast impatience. He struggled to sit up. The resulting fire in his leg, and the giddiness of his head, sent him flat on his back again. Nevertheless the hope of walking gave him the will to make cautious attempts at exercising his legs and his arms as well at intervals during the day. Each movement left him weak and trembling, but he persevered. And when sailors brought the evening meal of haberdine and biscuits boiled together, he took his share and chewed on it vigorously, amazed that salt fish could be so tasty.

The next morning, with Mr. Sprague on one side and Duncan on the other, Ross made an attempt to stand. He could feel his head swimming as the two men raised him to a sitting position. He managed to get his good leg firmly on the deck, and tried to rise. Then the unwonted stress on the injured muscles struck like hot iron, and he collapsed, sweat streaming from every pore.

"Tomorrow we shall try again," Mr. Sprague said cheerfully.

"Aye, 'twill be better then," agreed Duncan.

Ross gritted his teeth. Did they think he was going to undergo such torture even one time more? They must have taken leave of their senses.

On the morrow, however, the pain of the day before had faded. When the trap door opened, Ross caught a glimpse of a bright day and a breath of fresh air. He would give anything to get out on deck into the crisp breeze and sunlight. And to do that he must learn to walk again. So once more he tried to stand. And this time he succeeded in gaining his feet, although only for a moment. But it was a start.

Each day, as soon as the captives had gone on deck, Mr. Sprague climbed down into the 'tween decks. Sometimes he renewed the bandage on Ross's leg. Other times he supported him while he attempted to walk over the tilting floor. And always they talked.

One morning the Englishman said musingly, "Consider for a moment how little difference there is between your voyage and mine."

For a moment Ross was struck dumb. Then he blurted, "But ye be a free man!"

"Yes, but we are both exiles from our natal lands."

It was true. Imprisonment or worse awaited them both should they return to England or Scotland.

"Aye, but ye maunna face indenture."

"No, but you will have the certainty of an occupation and habitation." Was there a hint of envy in the Englishman's tone?

"But ye be a gentleman of means."

"No more am I," said Mr. Sprague wearily. "The few coins in my pocket are my last, and less than enough to pay full passage for myself and my daughter." There was no denying the panic that underlay the words.

"How will ye pay, then?" Ross asked.

"By means of a loan when we reach Boston, if I am fortunate. And there I hope to find some way to put my abilities to profitable use, though the prospect is poor. My only practical knowledge is in the managing of an estate—and in a land that is largely Puritan, who will engage a Royalist?"

"Could ye not send to England for funds?" Ross pursued.

"My family's holdings have been confiscated by Cromwell," the Englishman said bitterly. "Not one farthing is left to my use. My daughter and I spent what little I had on my person before we reached London. The sum I realized from the sale of our mounts has brought us thus far." His voice held a faint tremor.

For a few minutes they were both silent. Ross could find no honest word of cheer, and he could not bring himself to give false comfort. There had been too much forthright talk between them.

"I'd gie a fair penny, had I ane," Ross said at last, "to ken what the New World is like. I hae nae acquaintance wi' it whatsoever."

"There have been tracts and books enough printed about its fine forests and fertile lands, although methinks the writers have painted a fairer picture than is true in order to lure new settlers."

"How many folk would ye say hae voyaged there?" Ross asked, thankful that Mr. Sprague had regained his usual composure.

"Vast numbers. During the period of the great migration, when the Puritan cause was at a low ebb, some thirty thousand left England. Some, of course, have returned now that their faction is in the ascendancy, but every year more people make the crossing. 'Tis said that land can be had there for a trifling sum, or free for the clearing."

"Land—free?" Ross could hardly believe his ears.

"An incredible prospect, is it not?" Mr. Sprague smiled. "In time you may hold title to lands in the New World, Ross McCrae."

"Dinna mock me," Ross begged. "Hae ye forgot that I shall be indentured for seven years?"

"No, I have not," Mr. Sprague said, suddenly serious. "Nor have I forgotten that after seven years have passed you will again be a free man. More than that, you will have learned something of the country, and unless you are more of a fool than I take you for, you will have looked about you and studied as to what you may undertake as your life's work. Indeed, if there is one thing I could envy you for, it is your future."

His future! Ross almost laughed aloud. But the Englishman spoke with such conviction that Ross ceased to scoff, and thought back over Mr. Sprague's words. Through the long hours of his convalescence he pondered what lay ahead. And the more he mused about it, the more inviting became the prospect.

At last, after a week of learning to walk, Ross determined to essay the climb to the open deck. With John Davison ahead of him, and Duncan behind to give him a boost, Ross managed the ladder's ascent.

Panting, he pulled himself up into the square opening, stepped awkwardly over the coping and looked around. He was in the steerage cabin which housed the stout whipstaff used for steering the *Unity*. Two sailors now held it firmly, brawny arms bared to the elbow, massive hands gripping the wooden stock.

To one side of the steersmen a door swung ajar. As Ross's roving gaze reached it, a young woman wrapped in a peacock-blue cloak appeared and put her hand on the latch.

Her light brown hair was wind-blown, and her cheeks were pink with sunburn. For a moment her eyes met Ross's.

Then she slowly, almost reluctantly, pushed the door shut, and there was only a weathered panel where she had stood.

The encounter had lasted no more than a few seconds, but Ross in that brief time felt a deepening desire to know this girl. He was aware of her courage; without it she could not have survived the flight with her father. There was more, too, that she possessed—a warmth and glow that must have heartened her parent through the weeks of their journey.

The next minute Ross summarily dismissed all thoughts of Joanna. There was no point in his thinking of her for even a moment. She was a lady, born and bred, and he but a limping, filthy prisoner. Small wonder she had closed the door. The mere sight of him must be enough to disgust a woman, to say nothing of the stench that clung to him.

Holding to the bulkhead, he hobbled past the capstan in the space beyond the steerage, and came out onto the open deck. There he leaned weakly against the rail.

The sky! He had forgotten how vast it was! So long had he been cooped up in the 'tween decks that he had lost all remembrance of sunlight and puffs of cloud, and boundless reaches of blue.

Squinting, he stared at the sea. He could not have imagined the sheer expanse of it, stretching on and on to the horizon. Turning, he craned his head this way and that. On every side swelled blue-green billows. Where they rose and caught the sunlight, the color was the same as the girl's cloak. Sternly he checked himself. He must keep a closer watch on his thinking. As far as Mistress Joanna Sprague was concerned, he was but one insignificant part of the *Unity*'s miserable cargo. Better to keep his mind free of even the slightest thought of the girl than to torture himself with the impossible.

Now he filled his lungs with the clear, cold air. He could feel its chill deep down in his chest. And the brush of the wind on his face was more refreshment than he had known in weeks.

All too soon the time passed, and the Scots were ordered below. Struggling down the ladder, Ross saw Mr. Sprague standing near its foot. He reached out an arm which Ross took thankfully.

As they made their way toward the small area Ross occupied, the Englishman said sadly, "I fear that this is but the last time I may talk with you. When my daughter and I came aboard, Master Walker gave strict orders that we must keep aloof from his cargo, as he terms you. I importuned him to allow me to care for you while you were ailing. Now that you have mended, he insists that I have no more traffic with you."

Suddenly Ross became aware of the depth of his feeling for the older man. In a way he could never have anticipated, Mr. Sprague had been almost like a father to him. He would always think of this new friend as one who had continued the Laird's guidance.

"Then I'll ne'er hae e'en a word wi' ye again?" The prospect was almost more than he could bear.

"A master is sovereign aboard his ship," Mr. Sprague said ruefully.

All at once Ross was overcome by the remembrance of all that Mr. Sprague had done for him. "I canna gie ye proper thanks," he said miserably.

"One might say we have helped each other," the older man said slowly. He clapped one hand on Ross's shoulder. "I have no fear but that you will make the most of whatever lies before you. May God favor you in all your ways."

Ross was too choked to reply. Numbly he watched Mr. Sprague pass among the prisoners, shaking the hands of some, giving words of encouragement to others. Then he climbed the ladder, the trap door slammed shut, and gloom settled in.

Every day the 'tween decks seemed dark after the period when the Scots went up for their airing. Today the dusk seemed more thick and depressing than ever before. Others besides Ross must have felt a similar murk in their spirits. From dim corners came grumbling and cursing.

The ship, which had been rising and falling with a steady rhythm, soon began to toss jerkily. From above came the thunder of running feet, followed by the crack of canvas, and the shouting of men. Those white puffs of cloud were not as innocent as they appeared, thought Ross.

In the pitching 'tween decks the Scots were thrown to and fro. Their groans were interspersed with loud complaints.

"Be we to be shut up here for aye like sae many pigs in a pen?"

" 'Twouldna hurt the captain to let us hae a bit mair air. 'Tis fair stifled we be here."

"I'd rather hae died o' the flux at Durham than rot here in this stinking hole."

"Och aye! We'd be better off dead!"

Ross listened in growing anger. It was time that someone put an end to this interminable spewing out of resentment and dissatisfaction. Such talk was of no value and only made the situation more unbearable.

He listened, hoping that one of the older men would speak. Not one voice was lifted to turn the tide. Ross turned to Duncan. "Canna ye make them quit this sair scraichin'?" he asked.

"What recks it what they say?" Duncan asked. "We be all doomed, the lot o' us. Do we no' gae down wi' this ship, we'll but die in the New World."

Ross listened in amazement, realizing with a start how far away from Duncan and the others he had grown during his convalescence. Suddenly he was aware of the vast change that had taken place in his thinking in the past week. And he knew he must share some of his new-found hope.

"Hark ye," Ross cried in his lustiest tones. "Be this the talk of braw Scots? Can there be ane man amang ye whose heart beats no' the faster at the thocht of ane day havin' his ain land i' the New World?"

He might as well have spoken to the ship's wooden hull for all the notice the men paid to him. They kept on with their complaints in ugly voices.

Ross renewed his effort. "Hae ye no' heard that some free men and maids bind themselves to indenture o' their ain will that they may cross o'er to this new land? Glad they be to toil for seven lang years that they may gain their passage."

He paused, waiting for some comment. There was none. The men refused to listen to what they did not wish to hear.

As his anger grew, Ross knew again the same frustration he had felt in the cathedral when the two prisoners threatened to destroy the clock. He felt for his bagpipes and unwrapped them from their covering.

The feel of the mouthpiece was welcome to his lips. Its taste was as sweet as that of forbidden fruit—and as perilous. Augustine Walker was no man to let a prisoner retain anything that might arouse a feeling of patriotism among the Scots.

The danger intensified Ross's determination. All that mattered now was that he turn his comrades away from the self-pity that was festering in their minds.

Slowly, for he had not yet regained his full strength, Ross forced air into the sheepskin. He got shakily to his feet, nearly toppling as the vessel took a sudden lurch. Bracing himself between the hull and a stanchion, he got a firm enough footing, and settled the drones against his shoulder.

His fingers found their places on the chanter with a

sureness that made his heart knock against his ribs. He felt
almost as if Black Donald were guiding them as he had
that first day by the side of Loch Ruich.

Then Black Donald's voice sounded in Ross's inmost ear.
*Och, 'tis a strang weird that is laid on a piper. He canna gie
in to his ain sorrow, but maun e'er lift up the spirits o' the
clan.* With every quickening beat of his heart, Ross knew
that the strang weird had truly been laid upon him.

What matter that the men imprisoned with him in the
Unity's hold had come from various parts of the Highlands,
and from many clans? Their former differences had
dwindled to naught during the long, weary march from
Dunbar. Through suffering, privation, and exile they had
been fused into one body of Scots. It was time to put aside
old loyalties, treasured but of the past. He must consider
the present, and look ahead to the future.

These worn and weary men around him, drained of their
pride and vigor, were his clansmen now. With them he
had endured anguish such as few human beings would ever
know. With them he had come close to dying, and had
found a way back to life. He would never know how
greatly their care and concern had helped him to find that
way. Now was the time for him to act in their behalf!
His left arm pressed forcefully against the swollen bag. Out
rang a mighty challenging burst that might have been
Black Donald's. Ross could see men's heads turn and sensed
their growing attention.

He knew what he would play—the crowning glory of

Scottish music, a pibroch. As the notes poured from the pipes, Ross felt the pulse of destiny in his veins. Over and above the music came Black Donald's voice. *Many is the nicht when the Laird and our men hae sat doleful about the fire that the need has come o'er me to pipe out demons that plagued 'em—demons of fear and despair that hung in the blackness. There was need to pipe new heart into 'em, too, that in the morn they might rise up wi' new strength and courage.*

These grumblings and complaints, what were they but demons of fear and despair? What these Highlanders needed, as never before, was new heart. Of what lay ahead, and of what his own part in the future might be, Ross was uncertain. But for now he was Ross McCrae, the seventh in his line to pipe. And pipe new heart into his fellow Scots he would, so that in the morn they might rise up with new strength and courage.

Amid the storm and tumult, the young Scot drew music from the bagpipes. As he played he could feel new hope rising within him.

One thing Black Donald had not told him, he was discovering. When a man reaches into his own soul to give spirit to others, he finds a new and unexpected source of strength.

About
the author

MARY STETSON CLARKE was born and brought up in Melrose, Massachusetts, "in a book-loving family" who encouraged her early efforts to write. Following graduation from Boston University, she worked for four years on the *Christian Science Monitor*. After her marriage to Edwin L. Clarke, she lived near New York City, and studied writing at Columbia University while continuing to write feature articles for the *Monitor* and other publications. Except for the few years in the New York area, Mr. and Mrs. Clarke have lived in Melrose.

While her son and two daughters were in their teens, Mrs. Clarke began writing historical novels; and now that her family is grown, she continues to write for young people. Her books are noted for their intensive historical research. Her earlier novels include *Petticoat Rebel, The Iron Peacock, The Limner's Daughter,* and *The Glass Phoenix.*